ANGEL *Undone*

LETA BLAKE

An Original Publication From Leta Blake & Alice Griffiths

Angel Undone
Written and published by Leta Blake
Cover by Dar Albert
Formatted by Frostbite Publishing

First Paperback Edition, 2016

ISBN: 9781626227675

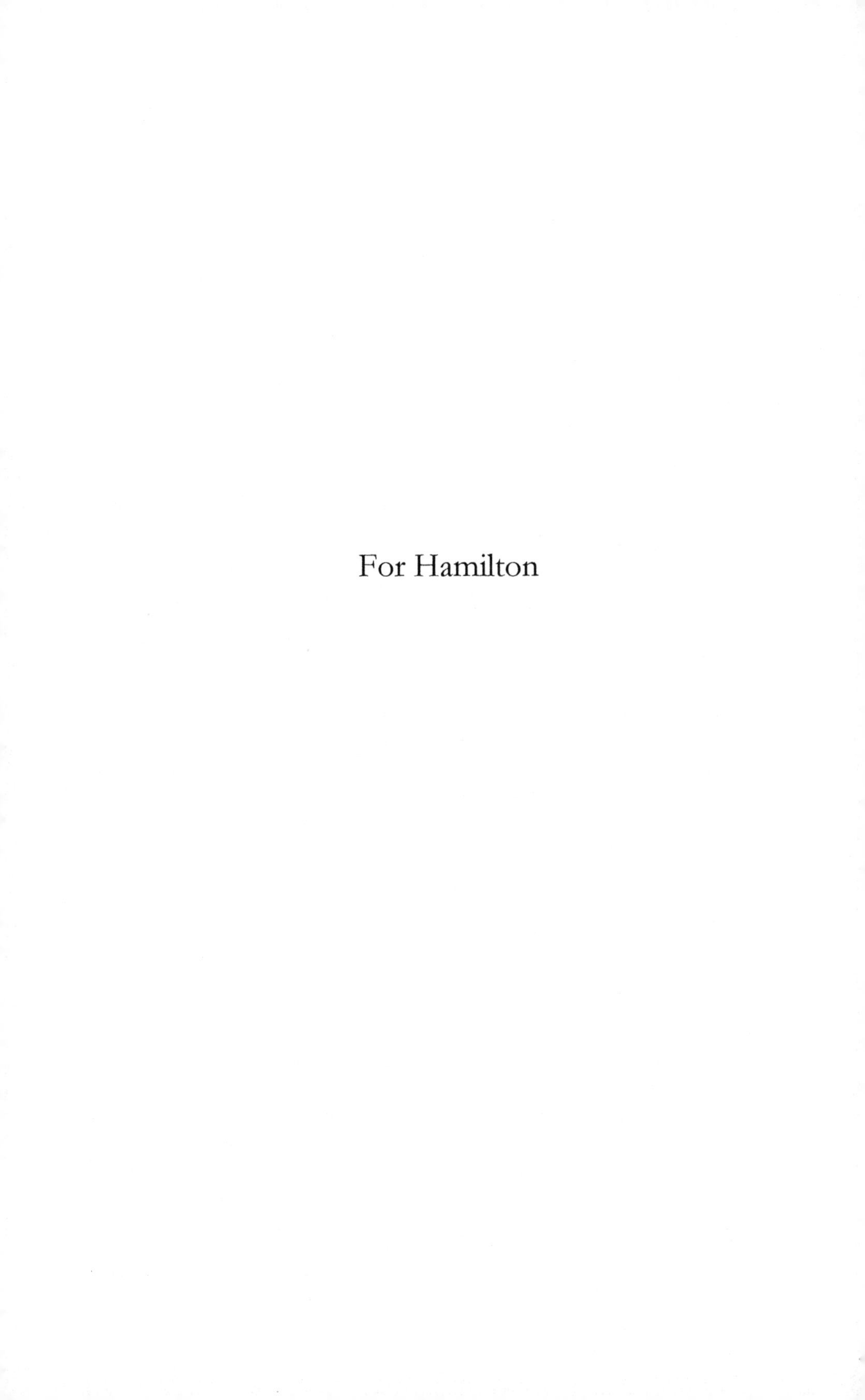

For Hamilton

ALSO BY

The River Leith
Smoky Mountain Dreams

The Training Season Series
Training Season
Training Complex

Co-Authored with Indra Vaughn
Vespertine

Co-Authored with AliceGriffiths
The Wake Up Married Serial

Gay Fairy Tales
Co-Authored with Keira Andrews
Flight
Levity
Rise

Free Digital Read
Stalking Dreams

ANGEL *Undone*

LETA BLAKE

ONE

Angel wings aren't easy to fold into the shape of human scapulae, but Michael is accustomed to the strain and hardly breaks a sweat. He forces the long primaries to bend into the upper wing coverts, and then, in moves like feathered origami, he tucks it all in again, before smoothing them under flawless human skin.

He glances in the modest hotel room's bathroom mirror and pulls on the dark brown shirt that will set off his eyes, before running a hand through his blond, curly hair. The light of his angelic grace glows from his pores, too bright to escape notice, and with a small exertion of will he tamps it back.

Though human form is confining and uncomfortable, the time has long passed when dropping down in a blaze of angelic righteousness was appropriate. Now covert operations pay the dividends of souls delivered from jeopardy. Even if Michael's skin feels too tight, and his wings are already aching, protection is his business and discomfort is a small sacrifice.

After tightening the laces on the leather, soft-soled Clarks he keeps for nights of trawling the Mercy Street bars, he kneels by the sliding glass door to the balcony and looks up at the stars. It's a fallacy that heaven is up there somewhere. Heaven is everywhere all at once, and yet when Michael dons human skin, he finds his eyes drawn to the sky when he prays.

He rises. Time to go.

All in all, angels aren't what they used to be. In the face of creation as it exists currently—suburbs, cities, cars, trains, and the vast sprawl of technology—dramatic entrances have been rendered obsolete, and as much can be accomplished with a misdirected email as a flashy herald from the sky. Angels' duties have shifted accordingly.

Protection is Michael's calling. Once, he was a warrior and his role a valiant one in an epic clash with great stakes, but heaven has been different since the war and there is no army to lead. As the ages drag out, it seems that there may never be a need for a heavenly army again. But Michael's desire to protect the people of God hasn't changed.

It's never the same victory twice. The mark is sometimes a woman, sometimes a man, occasionally a child, and protection can be hidden in a handkerchief given at just the right moment, a steadying hand across a busy street, a drive home on a night of too many drinks, or safe delivery to a house away from hands that hurt small bodies. But, occasionally, a desperate soul requires something more intimate than that.

Tonight his mark is sitting in a corner booth of Boat Out Bar at the very end of Mercy Street. With his head nodding gently to the loud strumming guitar of canned country music, and a clutter of beer bottles around him, the man plays host to a deep sadness that penetrates his bones. Michael drops onto a bar stool and orders a scotch and soda. The alcohol won't touch him, but the scent of it on his breath can suggest camaraderie to the drunken human he'll be approaching.

Michael examines his quarry closely—forty years old with dark, crescent-shaped marks of sleeplessness and recent tears under his eyes. His slim form is slumped forward, wrapped up in a long, dark trench coat, as if trying to disappear into its depths. His limp, black hair has seen neater days, and his dark eyes are rough with grief. He clutches another beer bottle with trembling, long fingers.

Michael peers harder, sees straight into the man's delicate, beating heart, feels around in the tight fiber of his muscle and discovers his name—Asher—along with the secret pain knit into his being. He closes his eyes, gasping softly as he presses deeper. Asher is an echo of the ocean several streets over: deep and teeming with hidden life. Each breath is a tide churning with unexplored emotions. Michael rubs a hand over his mouth. Like the tide, Asher's soul tugs at him.

Careful now.

Michael settles himself with a sip of his drink and then another, waiting for the sign that it's the right moment to approach. In the meantime, he glances over the room, looking for the danger. He's not sure if it's a person, a mood, or a thing, but he's never given a human to protect without *something* on its way. Given the way beer bottles are collecting on his table, it occurs to Michael that the danger might be inside the man himself.

As more beer goes down the hatch, Asher's eyes roam. They linger on a light-haired, tall man by the window and then steal away, frightened, when the tall man makes a gesture asking to cross the room to join him.

Asher keeps his eyes down and Michael can hear the thrum of his pulse, the subtle vibration of the internal words he uses to urge himself on: *Don't be such a sissy. Ha. Sissy.* ***Be*** *a sissy, Asher, come on. Just look at him. Just* ***look*** *at him.* Asher's eyes dart up again, and his lips tremble into a terrified smile.

Michael's attention turns to the man at the window. He narrows his gaze, takes in his heart, the breath that exits his strong lungs and penetrates farther into his bones, his marrow, his soul. There's a good person in that body—someone with a generous portion of mirth and humor, someone who loves children and small dogs. There is also too little patience, not enough self-control, and Michael downs the rest of his drink in one gulp before slapping some dollars onto the bar. This is his cue.

It takes effort to open his pores up just enough for a gentle glow to shine through. The eyes of men and women in the room suddenly focus on him, and he modulates his inner light, until they all turn back to their drinks and companions. All except for Asher, who now stares at Michael with glossy-eyed drunken wonder, as though he's just seen an angel—as though he knows, somehow, that he truly has.

Michael walks confidently toward Asher's booth, and slides into the darkness opposite him without asking permission. Asher's mouth is open, his lips wet and his tongue against the roof of his mouth.

"Are you driving tonight?" Michael says, smiling softly, allowing more light to illuminate his eyes. "I think you've maybe had too much to drink."

Asher's throat clicks as he swallows. It seems to take an effort to pull his gaze from Michael, but when he does, there's surprise in his expression as he takes in the table of beer bottles, and the one clutched in his hand.

"Wow," he says. "Look at that."

His voice shivers up Michael's spine, deeper and gentler than he expected.

"I think you've been at it quite a while." Michael grins and leans forward, taking hold of the neck of the beer bottle in Asher's hand and tugging gently until Asher lets go.

Asher takes a shaky breath, his bones screaming his anxiety.

Michael's chest aches in sympathy and he quickly eases Asher down, gracing his bones with a sense of holy safety. "Let me take you home. Make sure you get there safe and sound."

Asher rubs a hand over his face, and peers at Michael again. Asher's wide eyes set off an unexpected ricochet inside, like a pinball machine in Michael's normally calm chest. His job is to keep Asher safe, but he can't deny the man's ocean-soul is calling to him. He leans into it, wanting to illuminate Asher's depths with his own grace. *Careful, Michael.*

Asher's appealing voice is low-pitched and too quiet, but Michael hears it clearly over the clanking of glasses and the loud chatter around them. "I don't know. I mean, I don't even know you."

Michael takes a swig from the beer he's just liberated, suffuses peace into Asher's throbbing heart, eager to relieve him of anxiety, and settles back into the leather booth. He admires Asher's dark eyes, and allows a whisper of his attraction through too. "We could remedy that problem if you want."

Asher clearly misses Michael's cheesy innuendo and his shoulders relax from where they are bunched up by his ears. "Yeah. I'd like that. What's your name? I'm Asher, by the way."

"Michael," he says, putting his hand out.

Asher takes it with a delicate touch that sends a shiver through Michael. His skin flushes and a little radiance slips out. He won't have to work to give Asher what he'll need. Michael may be an angel, but he has preferences of his own. Sometimes he relies heavily on his ability to pull divine love through to the core of his angelic being while he gives the human he's helping what he or she needs. Tonight, though, he feels so much for Asher already, it won't require effort from him.

"Nice to meet you, Michael." Asher's dark eyes roam the table in front of them. "Wow, these bottles are staring me down like a row of accusers, all of 'em screaming, 'You're drunk.'" He flushes, embarrassed, and rolls his eyes. "Shit, ignore me. You're probably wondering why you even sat down now."

"You *are* drunk," Michael says. "We're in a bar. It seems the place for it. Nothing to be embarrassed about."

"Can we just—here—" Asher starts moving the bottles aside,

trying to get them out of the way, but he's uncoordinated and he nearly knocks the lot of them over.

Michael grabs several before any fall and break, stands up, and takes them to the trashcan by the bar. Once the table is clear, he sits down again across from Asher who's shored himself up against the side of the booth, his eyes glimmering with heat as he watches Michael move. An attractive form is always an advantage, and Michael's human body is decidedly beautiful. He chose the details himself—straight nose, full lips, curly blond hair, and soft, brown eyes. Beautiful, but not terrifyingly so. It's a combination that always does the trick.

He smiles at Asher. "There, they're out of the way. Feel better now?"

"Yes. Thanks. For cleaning up after me, I mean."

"It's not a chore."

"*Why* are you being so nice?"

Michael shrugs. "Because I saw you eyeing that other guy and I'd love it if you spent the night with me instead."

"I just met you and that's kind of…" He trails off, eyes wide, scared and excited. Mostly excited.

"But you were going to go home with him, weren't you?"

"Maybe? I might have chickened out. Probably would've actually."

"And if you hadn't?"

Asher wipes a hand over his mouth, his fingers trembling. "I'd have done it, at least. And I'd have to live with myself. Admit it. Admit what I am. Finally." Fire blazes in Asher's eyes and it starts to fade out almost as soon as it catches.

Michael reaches out, takes hold of Asher's hand where it rests against the table. He feels his responding attraction like a burning tingle against his skin. An answering flame grows inside, a desire to cover Asher with his wings, protect him, love him whole. "I can help you with that. In fact, I'd like to."

"Why? You don't know me."

"Maybe it's easier that way. You didn't know him, either," Michael says, an urge to draw Asher close flaring in him. "Or we can go back to remedying that problem."

Asher doesn't pull his hand away, but he doesn't speak either. The air between them pulses gently.

"Where should I begin?" Michael asks, biting his lip and basking in the glow of mutual burgeoning desire.

"How old are you?"

"I'm older than I look."

"Thank God, because you look half my age."

Michael ignores that. "I like baseball and chess. I enjoy movies with asinine fart jokes because my everyday life is pretty much always serious business. I prefer Coke to Pepsi. I find disaffected Jews attractive."

Asher cracks a smile.

"I believe you fit that bill."

"Does my nose give it away?"

"Does it matter? What else do you need to know before you agree to let me leave with you tonight?"

"Are you in school? Or do you have a job?"

"I work for my father," Michael says. "He runs a rather large business—a worldwide thing—very corporate. Very dull."

"Posh?"

Michael grins. "Don't I wish." He remembers the war and the subsequent years of rebuilding and the seeming eons of daily service to humans. "No, for the most part I work in the trenches."

"And your dad? Does he work alongside you? Are you close?"

No one is really close to Father. Not like that, anyway. "My father expects a certain respectful distance."

"What kind of business is it? What does he do?"

"It's complicated and rather vast."

"You said it's worldwide?"

"Yes, and very boring," Michael reiterates, letting off a little light to shut down further curiosity in that direction. "Father oversees the whole, great machinery of the thing, while my brothers and I travel and do the dirty work. What about you? What do you do?"

"I'm a professional at letting people down. If I could get a salary for that, I'd be set. Alas, if I got a salary for *anything* I wouldn't be letting my folks down anymore, so that'd be against the terms of my position. It's a damn Catch-22, I tell you."

Michael squeezes Asher's hand. It's a good sign he hasn't pulled away from him yet. "Charming sense of humor, my friend, but aren't you being too hard on yourself?"

Asher's expression is withering. He doesn't respond.

"All right. So, you're out of work. It happens to the best of us." Well, not really to Michael, but he supposes his brother Lucifer had been without a job until he'd carved himself out a nice position as the Prince of Darkness.

"I've never been in any kind of work to be out of. I went to school until I couldn't anymore. After that I took care of my grandmother until she passed away. Now? According to my father, I'm useless. I'm too lazy to get a job, or hold down a fort, or even set up a damn tent to keep myself out of the rain. My mother and I are close, but I know she's disappointed in me too. She just loves me too much to say so."

Michael doesn't think Asher would have even needed to chicken out had the fellow by the window made his way over. He'd have run him off with this line of conversation. "I'm not going to walk away until I know you've gotten home safely, so feel free to say all the disparaging things about yourself that you'd like."

"Why do you care?"

"It's what I do."

"Caring about strangers in bars is what you do?"

"Tonight, caring about you is what I do."

Asher pulls his hand away and slumps back against the slick vinyl of the booth. His eyes focus fully on Michael for the first time, a sober gleam beginning in them. "Why aren't you creepy? I should find you creepy."

"Because I'm not." He misses Asher's fingers, and he reaches out for them.

"See? That—*that* should be creepy. I should be entirely disturbed by you right now." Asher's hand slips into his own again, and Michael shivers, feeling a little more eager than he should. "You come over to pick me up, and when I'm a freak, you don't go away. I'm drunk, so I have an excuse. But, you're not. Or are you?"

"No, I'm not drunk." And Asher has a point. What is it about his vulnerability, his social awkwardness that makes Michael want to cuddle him closer than his average mission? Why does he want to comfort Asher to satisfy himself and not Father alone?

"So, what's wrong with you?"

"Oh, where to start with that question?" Michael deflects. "I have a particular weakness for Jewish men. I've mentioned that already. But, let me ask, why are you trying to scare off the same men you'd like to screw?"

Asher blinks rapidly, licks his lips, and says, "So, you came over here because you want to screw me?"

"Yes." Michael is surprised by how much *want* plays a role already. It often does once the time comes, but he's here to protect Asher from making a terrible mistake, not get off on his mission. And yet Asher's vulnerability is stirring something deep inside him. It makes no sense—vulnerability is on display before him every moment of every day, and yet something about Asher's dark eyes makes his cock thicken.

"I don't get it. You saw me over here, in a corner and you thought, 'I'd like to screw him'? So you came on over and asked to take me home?"

"I believe that's how it's done."

"Is it?" Asher sounds at a loss now, desperate and worried. "Is that how it's done? With girls it's…it's never as simple as…it's not like that."

"It depends on the girl," Michael says, taking another swig from the beer he stole from Asher. "But usually, no, it's a bit different for women than it is for men."

"Why?"

"The stuff our fathers taught us about them, the things their fathers taught them about themselves, the lives their mothers lead, the lives their grandmothers led. Culture. History. Religion. It all adds up."

"My father taught me *this* was wrong. Two men together."

"Your father and my father should meet. They'd probably have a lot to say to each other."

"But if it's wrong—"

"I never said it was wrong."

"—how can it feel so right? And how can you be so easy? A look across the room, and then you ask to take me home." Asher's lashes fall to his cheek. "What do we do when we get there?"

Michael's dick throbs and lengthens down his pant leg as he imagines how beautiful it will be to witness Asher awakening to his lusts, and he surrenders to the unusual thrill of helping him accept them.

Asher's voice is breathy. "How does this work? Would we fuck? Do we even kiss?"

Wondering what Asher's soft, drunk-loose mouth will taste like, he moistens his own lips in anticipation.

Asher leans forward, his heart pounding, and his pupils dilating. "Would you take me to my bed, or just fuck me on the stairs, or on the sofa, or the floor?"

"What would you want me to do?"

"I'm not the one auditioning here." He smiles wryly, flirtation floating over his face. "You're seducing *me*, remember?"

"That was my answer, Asher. I'd do whatever you wanted me to do."

Asher's heartbeat quickens and Michael's pulse thrums. Human flesh is so responsive. A sharp surge of want pierces him as Asher says slowly, "But I want to hear what *you* want to do. To me."

What he wants? It's never even a question. He does Father's

bidding and he protects humans. There's rarely room to indulge his own desires.

Michael tilts his head and studies Asher's eyes, the vulnerability twisting in them despite the demands of his words. As Asher's gaze darts away, he seeks deeper, finding the hum of anxiety and fear, hearing the murmur *could be a rapist*, and the hungry denial of lust. It's a wound he wants to heal, a sweetness he wants to pull up and nurture. Yes, Asher is a flower and Michael wants to watch him bloom. The image flushes him with desire and the words come easily.

"I'd kiss you while I undress you."

Asher's lashes flutter and his cheeks darken.

"I'd take my time with your mouth, find out what you like—gentle and slow, or rough and insistent." Michael flicks his tongue out to wet his bottom lip and Asher's eyes follow the movement. "I'd kiss your chin and your eyelids while I unbutton your shirt. I'd listen to your breath—does it hitch when I touch my lips to your collarbone, or do you like it better when I kiss just behind your ear?"

Asher sits very still, his pupils dark, and his lips parted, staring at Michael helplessly. He spins his words with a warmer energy, letting them pass to Asher and fill him. "I'd slip your pants off, but leave your boxers on, and then I'd ask you, 'Do you want my clothes on, Asher, or off?' and you'd say—"

"Off. I'd say I want them off."

Michael shudders with pleasure at Asher's insistent tone. "Good. I'd start with my shirt, too. Undo the buttons all the way down. I'd unzip my pants and slip them off. You'd see I'm not wearing underwear."

Asher gasps.

"By that time I'd be hard. Is it okay if I'm hard from kissing you and seeing you naked?"

"Yes," Asher says softly.

It feels so good to talk about what he wants, to imagine Asher's reaction to it all. The freedom adds an extra sweetness to his lust.

"Is it okay if I'm hard now telling you what I want?"

The click in Asher's throat is loud as he swallows and nods his head.

"I'd leave my shirt on my shoulders, something for you to take off later if you want, but I'd leave it so you'd know I'm not pushing you." He'll never push Asher. He'll only make it so good for him. So good for them both. The way Father intended sex to be.

A well of joy warms his gut, a protective heat that he'll share with Asher, healing him, making him whole. Tonight, he'll prepare him for a future where love can find him. A curl of jealousy slips up into his gut, confusing and unacceptable. He lets it slide away, hoping Father doesn't notice it. "It's up to you decide how far we go tonight, Asher."

"I'm so drunk. I'm not sure I can get hard. I should be hard right now."

Michael thinks he's picking up the slack, his cock full and balls tingling. He normally doesn't get carried away by his own seductions, but Asher is delicious in a way he can't resist. He considers reaching out to Father, ask him why Asher's like a tide pulling at him, but he doesn't want to lose his chance to feel this. Whatever the reason, he's willing to go under with Asher's tide, see how it feels to surrender to it.

"Who wants to screw a limp-dicked drunk?"

Michael wants to rub his hands all over him, shoving away the layers of sadness and guilt, revealing the soul beneath. He settles for squeezing his fingers. "It's okay. Let's say you don't get hard, Ash. I'll hold you, kiss your mouth, and touch your nipples with my tongue."

"Oh, God."

"I'll touch you everywhere and I'll let you explore my body with your hands and mouth." Michael wants to transport them to a bed now. "I'll rub my hard dick against your hip, but I won't come—"

"I want you to come."

"Then I'll come for you."

"Please."

Michael smiles and rises the table. "Do you want me to take you home now?"

"Yes," Asher whispers, letting Michael tug him up. "I want you to take me home."

TWO

Michael isn't surprised when Asher balks at giving his address. It's a smart move, really, not letting a stranger know where you live, so Michael lets him off the hook by suggesting they go to his hotel. This is why he keeps a room, after all.

It's impossible to know on any given night if the room will come in handy, but sometimes it does. Such as the nights when Michael has brought in homeless men or women for a shower and a set of clean clothes. Or the nights when a battered family requires a place to hide before making a clean break from town with providentially provided cash and a shot of heavenly confidence. But it isn't often he uses it for seduction purposes.

"It's clean," Michael says. "That's about all I can say for it."

Asher stands by the curtains gazing out the window. The view is unremarkable, but Asher looks out searchingly. He's sobered up some during the short walk from the Boat Out Bar, and his anxiety is of a more solid variety. Michael picks up the deep hum of it in

Asher's bones and he listens to it as he turns back the burgundy and blue covers on the queen-sized bed, giving Asher space.

"You come here a lot?" Asher says, his voice just barely louder than the in-room air conditioner.

"When I'm passing through on work, it's a place to sleep."

"Oh."

"I don't bring a lot of men here, if that's what you're asking. Well, not for sex, anyway."

Asher remains silent, his fingers curling into the fabric of the drapes, and his heart beating rabbit-fast.

Michael sits down in the square, blue-upholstered hotel room chair by the round little table in the corner, and removes his shoes, untying them carefully, taking his time. "You don't have to be scared. I'm very good at this, very patient and willing to hold back, to be kind." And he *is* good at it. While statistically sexual seductions account for a low number of missions in the scope of his work, over the centuries he's become well acquainted with the pleasures of the human body and the art of sex.

"My virginity is that obvious." Asher isn't asking, and Michael doesn't point out Asher nearly said as much back at the bar.

It's his experience that focusing on details like that loosens his grip on the bigger picture of gaining his assigned human's trust, pulling him in, and delivering salvation up to his father. Michael sighs, mentally acknowledging his father's 'salvation' changes from one day to the next and often from person to person. He's given up trying to follow his father's logic—or as he tends to think of it, his father's whims—long ago.

Michael leans back in the chair and watches the long line of Asher's back as he stares out the window. He gives him time to sort out what he wants.

Sex is a pleasure that at least makes stuffing himself into human skin enjoyable. The human body is built for sexual congress and the gratification of using it for that purpose is immense. He's never dared to say it aloud or let his mind form the thought into a confessional prayer, but he enjoys the experience of human lust and orgasm more than almost any other sensation. Almost more than being naked and submissive in his father's presence, and that is considered by humans and angels alike to be the most blessed and rewarding experience of all.

Blasphemy.

Michael hears in Asher's heartbeat the moment his determination overtakes his fear. As Asher jerks the drapes closed, shutting out the reflected light of street lamps bouncing against the brick wall outside, Michael spreads his legs to welcome Asher into the space between them. Asher stands looking down with his grief-rough eyes, and he whispers, "Tell me why I should trust you."

Michael twines his fingers with Asher's soft, cool ones. "Because you're fighting a battle and you need someone on your side. Living this lie—it's killing you from the inside out, Ash."

"I don't want to live a lie any longer, but my father…"

"I've been in my fair share of brutal and bitter fights—" he's been nearly pulled into hell by his own brother after all "—so, where you are right now, battling for your life and what is right for you, feeling like it's your father's love on the line—I've been there, too."

"Your father didn't accept you?"

"My father is the most judgmental man you'll ever meet and I live every day in dread of him."

Michael remembers Lucifer's face aglow with righteous rebellion. An answering fire sparks inside him, held tightly wrapped in confining human skin. Is it any wonder orgasm is such a glorious thing? The intense and all-too-fleeting sensation of breaking free of the prison of the human body, the delicious pleasure of escape that seems, in the moment, worth almost any consequence?

Oh, Lucifer, look how you tempt me even now with your example. Is it so very dark without our father's love?

Michael has never dared to ask. He isn't sure he could trust Lucifer to tell the truth anyway.

But he can tell the truth to Asher.

"You can trust me on this, at least—you can lose your father, Asher, but gain a life of your own. The loss is immense but the reward is nothing short of fulfilling your destiny."

"You'll be gentle."

"Yes."

"You won't hurt me."

"No."

Asher grips Michael's fingers tightly, and with a grim paleness to his cheeks, he drops to his knees, his face aligned with Michael's groin, and he licks his lips. A tremor runs through his body, and he doesn't let go of Michael's hands, gazing up with wide-eyed terror.

"Let me suck it."

Michael feels a tight clench of lust spike through him. Even inexperienced, Asher's mouth will be hot and wet, and if there are teeth—well, Michael's always been a little bit of a masochist. He pulls his hands loose and undoes his button fly, watching Asher's face grow heated as his cock is revealed.

It's a pretty one. Michael chose a long, rosy length with a reasonable girth, but nothing a virgin like Asher will be too terrified to take in hand…or ass. As for the head, Michael always chooses circumcised. There is the whole thing with Abraham and his covenant with Father to consider when designing a human body. He's happy he doesn't have to endure the act itself, but simply fashion a penis that fits his father's whimsical orders.

Asher makes a noise at the sight and all hesitation is thrown to the wind. Permission to act on his urges seems to overwhelm him, and he's greedy as Michael shoves his pants down far enough that his cock bounces free. Asher's mouth is on it before Michael settles back into his chair, and, yes—hot, wet, enthusiasm with an edge of teeth that makes him yelp.

Pain can be a wonderful thing—underrated by far too many humans as far as Michael can see, but he supposes that's to be expected when the submissive perfection of the angelic state is unknown to them.

"Shh, slow, slow," Michael murmurs. Despite his own willingness for a dash of discomfort in the mix, he knows he needs to lay the groundwork for future encounters. "Take your time. Watch the teeth. Use your hand."

Asher gets a grip at the base of Michael's cock and it's just that much better now. He relaxes, leans his head against the back of the chair and lets Asher have at it. It's sloppy, and there's a lot of spit sloshing between Asher's fist and his mouth, sometimes rushing down over Michael's balls. It's nice, good—not the best Michael's ever had, but over centuries the delicious details all blur together. It's enthusiastic and that's what he always likes most.

Finally, Asher pops off, his lips red and wet, his eyes glazed over and pupils blown wide. "Wow," he whispers, licking the head of Michael's cock again, tonguing the slit, and sliding his mouth over the head to suck. Another pop off and he's panting now. "Wow. I knew I'd love it…but, God—wow."

Michael's game for letting him suck for as long as he wants. His skill level and lack of dedication to a rhythm makes it unlikely Michael's going to have trouble lasting to the next phase, but Asher seems to have another plan. He stands abruptly and ditches his shirt and his pants while Michael slowly strokes his cock, watching.

Long, lean legs with black hair against pale skin, lead up to a thick, veiny cock that's bigger than Michael's by far. It takes a moment for Michael to pull his eyes away from it. So many new images fill his mind, most featuring himself on his stomach with his ass in the air. Because that cock was made to plow, he's sure of it, and if anyone can handle the discomfort of something that big in the hands of someone so inexperienced, it's him.

"Wow, yourself," Michael murmurs, and is pleased when Asher takes his huge prick in hand to pump it, showing off. The shyness is gone now. It always amazes Michael how quickly a mouth full of cock can change things.

Michael kicks his pants free, and unbuttons his shirt, leaving it on for Asher to remove later as he'd promised in the bar. "Bring that gorgeous prick over here."

Asher does as he's told, stepping back into the space between Michael's knees. He holds his cock against Michael's mouth and rubs the slick head over his lips, smearing his pre-come on like ill-applied Chapstick. Michael lets him play, keeping his mouth shut as Asher drags his cock against Michael's cheek, gasping at the scratchy stubble, and over Michael's eyebrows, down his other cheek, and to his mouth again.

Michael grabs hold of Asher's hips and remembers his training ages ago in a series of brothels he worked in Sodom. Those were days of adolescent heights of sexual obsessions. His work included forays into it almost every day. Then the rapes happened, followed by retribution and destruction, and, well, sexual salvation assignments grew less frequent in the following ages.

Michael opens his mouth and sucks Asher's cock in deep and fast, taking it into his throat, letting it slide back out. Asher groans, tossing his head back and tensing all over. It seems unfair to do this to him, take him from zero to oh-my-God-is-this-real? He's not going to get this sort of treatment from most guys, Michael knows. It's been a few years since his mark was a virgin and a man, but he usually takes it slowly, sucking the head and bringing them off with a pumping hand and rhythmic suction.

But something about Asher's enthusiastic, messy attempt has him wanting to escalate to the hottest, fastest, most intense place he can. Or maybe it's just been too damn long since he got to screw a guy with a flat stomach and a handsome face. Or maybe it's something about Asher's flesh and bones and the anxious, needy hum that feeds into Michael's own, singing with *so good, so **good**, oh, please, God, so **good**.* Regardless, Asher's a blithering maniac now, spilling filthy words that imperfectly echo his body's pleas.

"You—oh, God, you're gonna make me! I can't stop, can't stop—it's so close, aw, fuck, *fuck*, your mouth, your fucking *mouth*—" His hips twitch and thrust, and Michael grips them hard, holds him steady, moving his head so Asher's cock is fucking his throat, and just as he's going to spill, Michael pulls back, tonguing the slit and jerking his hand wetly on Asher's dick in a fast, urgent rhythm.

His own cock thrums against his stomach, aching for a touch, yearning for the return of Asher's mouth, but it can wait. He's bringing Asher careening into the finish now, and he spares a glance up to see Asher's chest heaving and stained red with exertion and lust. He's beautiful with his dazed eyes and his sparse chest hair swirling in tufts around dark, small nipples. Michael's suffused with affection and pride. "That's it," he encourages before going back to sucking. "You're being so good for me."

Asher covers his face with his hands, and Michael doesn't stop sucking to tell him not to be ashamed, to let him see, because this is Asher's moment. A rushing connection opens between them, angelic and human twining together, and Michael pushes his own arousal into Asher's body, too.

Asher's torso tightens, his breathing stuttering. As his cock swells in Michael's hand and the first white, hot load of semen spurts onto Michael's tongue, he throws his arms wide and cries out. His wild eyes pin to Michael's, his flesh and bones screaming *yes, yes, for* ***you***. He convulses as he pours his pleasure out.

Through their connection, the ecstasy hits Michael hard, loosening his grip on his human skin. A flash of light pulses in the room as Michael's cock throbs and shoots untouched. It's a shocking orgasm that rolls through him. He pulls Asher closer, shaking and trembling as his chest and shirt are drenched with his own come, all while milking twitching, shocked cries of lingering pleasure from Asher.

Fuck, Michael thinks. *Holy fuck*. It's been a long time since he let a human's pleasure run so hard into his own. It's exciting. It's beautiful. He knows his father will probably cluck his tongue and disapprove. Michael has a function, but damn if he can remember it right now with his human skin barely containing him, his wings itching in the confines of human scapulae, and his body ringing with shared and amplified satisfaction.

He kisses Asher's cock, and stands up, helping the now-limp man toward the bed, where he collapses face down, still quivering with aftershocks. Michael sits beside him, his hand resting on Asher's panting back. He looks at the come on his own stomach and chest, and closes his eyes, shuddering. Not since his affair with that beautiful, nervous, but incredibly delicious dolt in Queen Elizabeth's court has he gotten carried away enough to lose control that way. He wonders if Asher noticed or if he just assumed it was the intensity of his orgasm that caused the flash of light.

"Christ," Asher mumbles against the sheets.

Michael almost jokes that he's not nearly so humble as that particular fellow, but he can't bring himself to speak just yet. It's been so long.

Michael sheds his human skin and returns to the steady submission of angelic state. He's put it off as long as he could, and had it not been for Henry's sweet mouth, Michael would have shed his body days before.

At the thought of Henry, Michael plots his return. The next assignment he has. Surely a detour to the court will not be noticed or condemned?

At that moment, his father calls to him, and Michael redirects his steps to the Throne of Thrones. As always, it is impossible to look upon his father, and finds himself prostrate on the floor in naked submission.

"You, Michael, are getting too near to him," his father says, his tone bored with the infinity of all knowledge.

Although no name is spoken, Michael knows Father means Henry.

"I'm fulfilling the assignments you give, Father," Michael says. "Queen Victoria did not drink the poison. The barber did not bleed the young duke to death. Is it so bad that I see him, too? Can these things not exist side by side?"

"Your assignment was to save Henry from his fear of his own nature, not to indulge in an endless episode of altogether unangelic lusts. I know, Michael, wearing a human form comes with pleasures to make bearable the pains."

Michael has to bow his head.

"I have never denied my angels exploration and enjoyment of the sensual side of humanity during their time in human skin, but there has always been a limit."

"Henry and I cannot reproduce as my brothers did with Eve's daughters."

"No, but this you do with him is becoming something more."

"I have not fallen in love."

"No, of course not. For you, pleasure with Henry is not about love. It is about yourself." He feels Father's smile and it is mostly benevolent. "Congress is a beautiful thing that brings the future for my children. I encourage it in all healthy expressions which befit a human's nature. It is not meant to feed an angel's dissatisfaction with his place in my creation."

The threat isn't spoken. It's not even a threat. Not to **Father**, who knows and sees and feels everything, so nothing is good or bad any longer. But to Michael, it's a threat.

Lucifer was dissatisfied, and look what has become of him. If Michael continues to see Henry, the sweetly shaped man with powdered hair and a body that makes Michael's human form sing in heretofore unknown pleasure, might he lose his place? Will he be cast down?

Michael doesn't dare ask.

He doesn't see Henry again. He doesn't allow himself to miss it. He enjoys, even wallows in the seduction assignments as they come, but stays focused on their salvation. He never again considers returning to the same man for a second night, or a third, or more.

Michael runs his fingers through the hair at the back of Asher's neck. He's still collecting himself from the unbearable freedom that crashed over him at orgasm. Angels are intended to be submissive and perfect. Humans are slaves to the trap of their body. But this *wonder* is true freedom. And when it's like it is with Asher—violently, exposingly urgent—it's addictive.

"Thanks," Asher says hoarsely. "I think I'm fucked now."

Michael whispers, "No. Not yet. Give me a few minutes and I'll see what I can do about that."

"No, no. I'm so *fucked*. How am I supposed to do anything now?" He rolls over, black eyes shining with emotion. "I didn't know. Michael, do you understand? I didn't *know*."

As he first discovered with Henry so long ago, Michael *does* understand. How humans ever get any work accomplished when Father allows them to share *this*, he has no idea. No wonder their church and culture have so twisted his father's words and creation in the attempt to put orgasm into a box.

"My hand? Nothing compared to this. Fuck. *Fuck*."

Michael nudges Asher over and collapses beside him, his shirt half off one shoulder. He breathes slowly, waiting for his skin to feel settled, because the memory of Asher's face as he came, the message in his body (*for* ***you***) has him half-hard again, and shot through with lust.

This is dangerous, he thinks. What is it about this sad, sweet little man living his desperate life—not unlike millions and millions of others of Father's creation—that makes Michael feel more than he should? He thinks of that human expression, of things that get under the skin.

Why, Father? Why did you send me to him?

Long minutes pass, as Michael sends the desperate question up in prayer, staring at the ceiling, imagining the night sky beyond it. Surely his father doesn't *want* him to fall? The air conditioner has cooled their sweat enough that Michael is slightly cold, and as he moves to crawl beneath the blanket, Asher does as well.

"Is it always—"

"No," Michael says. Because it's not. He's fucked untold men and women and only with Henry was it ever close to this.

"Why?"

"Chemistry," he says, but he thinks *souls*.

But he's an angel. He has no soul. Not like that anyway.

He can't explain it. He never could with Henry either. Asher is forty years old and an attractive man, but Michael's had sex with other men who were more stunning. *It's never looks*, he recalls telling a woman a few nights before, as she'd cried on his shoulder over losing the man she thought she loved, fearing it was her aging face that'd driven him away. *What makes a connection between two people is something only God knows or understands.*

Why did you send me to him?

"I came so hard I thought I'd died." Asher rolls onto his side, smiling unsteadily at Michael. "Was it okay? Did I do okay?"

Did he do okay? Here Michael is contemplating whether or not he could risk everything by seeking Asher out again tomorrow, and the next day, and for as long as he can before Father puts an end to it, or casts him to earth for good, and he wants to know if he did *okay*?

"You did great. It was great. I thought I was dying, too."

"*Le petite mort*," Asher says in accented French. His dimple is unexpected, and the happy glow in his eye feels as sweet as a kiss.

Speaking of.

Michael leans over and kisses Asher, tasting his tongue, sucking at his slippery lips, sharing the taste of Asher's come. He laughs when Asher realizes it, and instead of pulling away, dives in for more. It's delightful, and there's a weird pull in Michael's stomach to see Asher again. He should ignore it. But he thinks maybe he won't. Not this time. One more night can't hurt.

"Wow," Asher says again. "You're all…scratchy. It's good. This is good." He gestures between them. "It's really good."

"It is," Michael agrees. "You are."

Blessed be, it is so good. Michael's not sure when he was last fucked. It seems that in most cases, he's the one to do the fucking. But tonight, for Asher's first time, Michael's on his stomach, sweating, biting the pillow, and wondering if Father put the prostate just *there* because he's a generous deity or a horrible son of a bitch. It stops mattering when Asher rams into him hard and fast, jolting pleasure through him in arcs that threaten Michael's control.

"Damn, you're so tight. And hot," Asher says desperately. "God, how are you so hot?"

Michael spreads his legs apart, letting Asher go deeper, and he doesn't just see stars, he's *sweating* stars. He loses a little control and angelic light breaks in sparks over his skin. Asher's so far gone that he doesn't do more than stutter, "Holy shit, I thought fireworks were a joke."

Michael can't speak. His shoulder blades itch, and he forces his wings in tighter, the effort of which only makes him squeeze his ass around Asher's cock, and that's so good for both of them they cry out together. Chills break over Michael's body, and Asher grips Michael's hand, as he whimpers and mouths at the back of Michael's neck.

"You like my dick in you?" Asher's voice is ragged.

"Yes," Michael says. "You have no idea."

"Am I…am I doing it right? I am aren't I? Look at you."

Michael squirms on Asher's thick cock, feeling the stretch all over—in his nipples, in his eyeballs, racing over his scalp. He's so *big*. "It's perfect."

Asher moans and redoubles his efforts. Michael clings to his fingers, and rubs against the bed sheets, hoping to get some relief. It's been so many years since he felt this kind of immense physical pleasure, so long since someone else's natural urges and movements fit so well with his own.

Your own? He fights back the condemning voice in his head. You're Father's tool. You don't have urges and needs of your own.

But he does. And he always has.

"Michael, please," Asher says, a note of desperation in his voice. "I'm going to…I can't wait."

"Do it."

Asher doesn't let go of Michael's hands, hunching desperately into him. Michael's ass feels alive and desperate for more, gripping and releasing Asher's dick on each stroke.

"You're so beautiful, so hot and tight," Asher moans and twists, fucking into him as hard as he can. "Are you real? This is too good. I'm gonna—"

He feels the resonance the moment Asher reaches orgasm, welcomes the stutter of hips and breath, and the hard thud-thud of Asher's cock unloading into the condom, as Asher's body screams *yes, God, yes,* ***yes***.

Michael pulls his right hand free of Asher's and works it down to his own dick. It only takes a few tugs and he's coming again, too, clenching and grinding on Asher's cock.

They tremble and hold each other for a long time before Asher eases out, leaving Michael feeling wide open and aching. He rolls onto his back, intensely aware of the confines of his human body again after the jerking bliss of freedom he'd just tasted.

Asher lies next to him, staring up at the ceiling. Waves of excited satisfaction roll off him. Michael bites his lip, reveling in the sensations coursing through them both.

Asher grins. "Why did I wait so long?" He licks his lips. "Now what?"

Michael turns on his side, too, reaches out to touch Asher's face. "We have tonight. Anything you want."

"Just tonight?"

Denial flares inside. He doesn't want to admit that. He opts for a shrug.

"In case you're worried, if this is the part where people get clingy, I'm not going to do that. If this is just a one-time thing, I understand." He doesn't sound as if he really does, though.

Michael knows what he's supposed to say. He's done this so many times before. "If I say it's just for tonight, what will you do next? Will you go back to denying this to yourself?"

"No. Not ever again."

"Good." Michael wants to tell him that he'll meet him back here tomorrow night. He wants to say, "*Let's not get out of this bed for the next week.*" He wants things that aren't part of his mission.

"It might be fun to explore my options. Maybe the guy I had my eye on earlier tonight. Maybe someone else."

"It won't be as good," Michael says. It's true, but petty for him to say.

"Sure, that blow job was astounding, but—"

"No buts. It won't be as good."

Asher's eyes narrow suspiciously but he looks amused. "Are *you* getting clingy and possessive? I thought that was the prerogative of the inexperienced."

Is he? He isn't supposed to. "It's just the facts. You should be prepared. Not every guy you take home is going to spark with you like this."

"How many men have you sparked with? Like this?" Asher asks, his dark eyelashes fanning on his cheek.

Why is Michael noticing these things? He sighs, gazing into Asher for whatever is inside him that makes the sex so good, that draws Michael in. It's there, nameless, a kind of hum that Michael wants to lean into until he's enveloped by it. It's familiar and unique all at once. It's got Father's thumbprint on it. A blessing.

"Have there been lots of men you've felt this spark with?" Asher asks again.

"Just one. A very long time ago."

Asher scoffs. "You can't even be thirty years old. How long ago are we talking here?"

"I told you. I'm older than I look."

In all eternity there has only been Henry. Sweet, sexy Henry. A dolt, for certain, but Michael's human form had been set endlessly ablaze by him. Asher, at least, is intelligent.

"How old are you exactly?" Asher asks.

"Older than thirty."

Asher rolls his eyes. "Cryptic isn't cute."

"Not trying to be cute, my friend." Michael runs his thumb along Asher's cheekbone and tries to turn his attention to the matter at hand. Has he accomplished his mission yet? With any luck, he hasn't, and he can do something about the hard cock that has returned with a vengeance. "Is this everything you needed, Ash?"

"You mean in order to prove to myself this is what I want?"

Michael smiles softly. It's what Asher wants. He's got his Father's special stamp all over him, all over his bones and in his blood. Special delivery—one male with leanings against the predominant culture! *Enjoy your difficult life! Learn to love yourself, because I do!* Father is a son of a bitch, really.

Perhaps he should try to find out Lucifer's phone number, or at least where in the world he's living these days. Because his mouth is forming the words before he knows he's going to say them.

"Can I see you tomorrow?"

Asher grins, his dark eyes glittering. "Name the time and place. I'll be there."

THREE

Museums are good for contemplating the vastness of eternity. Michael tucks his hands in his pockets and stretches his shoulders. The itch of his wings is uncomfortable but he knows he'll get used to it. He stares at the painting of *The Archangel*, admiring the attention to detail in the wings.

"Hello," Asher says, his voice low and smoky. "I'm sorry I'm late. Traffic."

Michael turns to see Asher wearing brown pants, a green button-up shirt under a corduroy jacket, and scuffed Clarks. It's a nearly identical outfit to Michael's own, except that his shirt is yellow and his pants are navy. Michael seeks inside Asher and finds that he actually overslept but he smiles and accepts the token of violets Asher extends.

"From our garden. My mother's favorite."

Traditionally violets stand for a delicate love, something fragile, fresh and sweet. Michael wonders if Asher knows that. The heightened color on Asher's cheeks and the bashful look in his eyes makes him think he does. He almost pushes into flesh and bone again to read it in him, but he chooses not to. Somehow, not knowing for sure makes it a little sweeter.

"They're lovely. Thank you." He puts one in the buttonhole of Asher's jacket, and tucks the rest behind his own ear, making a silly face as he does. Asher smiles and reaches out to pull them free and presses the stems carefully back into Michael's curly hair so they stay in place.

They stand and look at each other with smiles Michael can only call goofy. Asher's eyes no longer sport dark crescents beneath them and they seem to sparkle.

"You look good," Michael says.

"Thank you. So do you. You look amazing." He stumbles on, "I'm really sorry about being late. I realized I didn't have your cell number and was freaking out in the car. I was worried you'd leave and I'd never hear from you again."

Michael pulls the phone from his pocket and they share contact information. Asher is the first legitimate contact he's ever entered into the prop he uses only to appear typically human while on assignment. He swallows hard as he presses *Save As New Contact*. The act feels like rebellion.

"There. No more missed connections," Asher says and pockets his cell. His eyes rise to the painting before them and he sighs. "This is one of my favorites."

"Is it?"

"Yeah, my mom used to bring me here. She'd sit on the bench and look at *Astrid in Ecstasy*." Asher points at the painting on the opposite wall. "I'm not sure what she saw in it, but clearly it moved her. I would sit with my back to her back, and stare at this painting while I waited. I loved his wings."

"They are fine wings."

Asher seems lost in memory. "Eventually, I started to pray to Michael, The Archangel in the painting, to change me, to fix me. I gave in to the seductive idea that prayer helps." Asher laughs softly under his breath.

There's a strange pressure in Michael's throat and his eyes burn. He doesn't pay much attention to the prayers directed his way. There are simply too many of them and he's busy with his missions most of the time. Even for an angel, there's only so much he can do and it isn't his job to choose which pleas are answered.

All in Father's time, indeed.

"It's a common prayer."

Asher smiles painfully, his eyes still on the painting. "Last night, when you introduced yourself…" He shrugs and rolls his eyes. "It's silly. Never mind."

"Don't stop," Michael says, refusing to look inside Asher for the answer. "Tell me."

"I heard your name and for a moment I let myself believe that maybe my prayers had been finally answered."

"Did you?"

"Truth is, Michael, I still feel that way." Asher clears his throat and looks at his feet.

"Well, maybe that's the case, then. If we were meant to meet last night, who are we to go against God's plan?"

There's a justification now and he clings to it like he's seen humans cling to their excuses for just one more hit of their drug of choice. If Father knows what will happen, if he's planned this from the start, Michael's only doing what has been asked of him, isn't he?

"What about you? What do you like about it?" Asher nods at the painting.

"The wings," Michael says. "They're quite fine wings."

"Quite fine? You sound like someone's grandpa. From Britain."

"Britain has many fine grandpas," Michael says, laughing softly. It's a feeling like none other and one he doesn't get very often. Angels, for the most part, are serious creatures, and laughter is the medicine of humans.

"Come on, I'd like to see the Picasso. It's this way," he says pulling Asher away from the painting before he can give too much thought to the upper right corner of the canvas and its parting clouds unveiling a disembodied hand, finger pointing accusingly.

Over coffee in the museum café, Michael ignores the people who continue to look at him oddly for having flowers stuck in his hair. Instead, he listens to Asher talk about being adopted.

"It's just that I feel like I owe them, you know? They took me in when no one else wanted me. They loved me, or tried to love me, just the way I am. So now, I feel like I should take care of them. But I'm not sure they'll ever accept me." He sips his coffee morosely. It's not a good look on him, and Michael wants to reach out and wipe the expression off his face. "Take care of them? Who am I kidding? The first thing I need to do is find a job. In this market it's harder than it seems. Especially for someone without work history. A resume that consists of a PhD in European history and 'Ten years caring for aging grandmother until she died' doesn't make potential employers hot for me."

"You'll find work," Michael says with certainty.

"Maybe. Anyway, so, that's another reason I never left. My grandma was always so good to me. When someone saves you like that, when they love you on purpose, putting in that sort of effort and making those kinds of sacrifices, you don't show them disrespect by leaving them alone to rot and die in an old age home the way my dad wanted to do."

"Colorful."

He glances down at his coffee and fiddles with the handle. "I gave up so much to care for my grandmother and I've given up so much to try and be the son my parents want. But I *am* starting to hope maybe I can do both. Stay and be their son, and still have some kind of life of my own." He glances up at Michael and the heat in his eyes is echoed in a low, hot coil in Michael's groin.

Asher's ripe mouth, his black eyes, his timid hopefulness makes Michael want to take him apart with his angelic warrior strength, ravish him, and bring him to his knees with pleasure.

Asher licks his lips and smiles. "Do you ever want that kind of balance, Michael? In your life?"

Balance in his life? There isn't supposed to be balance, only mission and devotion to Father.

"Perhaps."

"Oh." He sounds disappointed, and Michael reaches out to touch his hand, stilling it on the handle of his mug.

"Now, I didn't mean it like that."

"How did you mean it?"

"I meant that I hadn't thought of it before. It's never been an option. But it's not that I don't like the idea."

Michael tilts his head and two of the violets fall into his coffee. Their laughter echoes in the empty café, drawing the attention of the barista. Asher doesn't flinch as the man looks at their joined hands, but Michael lets go anyway and takes up his sugar spoon to fish the flowers out of his drink.

Asher plucks the last violet from Michael's curls. It's wilted and limp. He puts it down on the table between them where it rests—purple, yellow, green. Shortly, the flowers from Michael's cup are arranged on the edge of his saucer, and the final one in Asher's buttonhole leans miserably to the side. He laughs again, stroking his fingers over Asher's hand. The softness of his skin and the knotty curve of his joints makes him go soft inside and so Michael does it again.

"I've enjoyed our date," Asher says. He leans back far enough that his hand is no longer accessible to Michael's fingers.

"I have too."

"But I'd feel a lot more comfortable if you weren't so young."

Michael doesn't protest. He can fix this by showing him the driver's license in his wallet. He can fix this by just telling him an age he can understand and will want to hear. Or by suffusing him with enough of his grace that he won't care anymore. But he doesn't. If this can be how it ends, if he can let it be over now without another tempting taste of Asher's body, then it must be for the best.

"At the same time, I don't think I'm ready to let this go. I don't want to go back to hiding from myself." Asher glances down, his thick, black eyelashes fanning on his cheek. It's becoming a familiar expression to Michael. He knows without having to seek it inside of him that Asher's going to confess something he finds embarrassing now. "And, I have to admit, every time I look at you I just want to find a bed and make good use of it."

Michael's groin tightens.

"The tiny one in the Elizabethan gallery looked plenty good enough to me if not for those hovering guards," Asher says quietly, his eyes darting to the barista, and back to his coffee, color rising on his cheeks. "So, right now, I feel like I should just say damn it all."

"Damn it all?" Michael swallows. He can feel the heaviness of the words like steel weights dangling from his balls, tugging at him with delicious, tempting pain. His wings itch, itch, *itch* under his skin.

Michael's mind goes to the Elizabethan era gallery on the second floor, too, but not to the bed. Instead, it lingers on a particular painting done by a relatively unknown artist hanging in the least advantageous position in the room. When he'd laid eyes on it, it'd rendered him speechless for several moments.

"Henry, darling, put the paintbrush down."

"I will not."

"Replacing her face with a dog's shall only lead you into peril should it be discovered."

"Nay, for I intend to burn it when I am quite finished."

"The Queen does not suffer fools lightly, Henry, and you are ever so foolish at times and now behaving rashly. It is not wise."

"I'll leave wise to people who have no heart. She had them put to death! They were but infants!"

"They were pups, Henry, and while you loved them dear, there were too many by far for the court. The Queen cannot harbor every bitch's brood."

"I say why not when she harbors the whores of the fancy Lords? Would my sweet Maiden's pups have not contributed more happiness to our court than the lot of those sluts?"

"Shush! Before the guards hear you. Your tears and wails have called them to your door. Who do you think fetched me?"

"You always come when I need you. I supposed you fetched yourself."

"Right you are, then, and I believe you should return the Queen's face to its lovely shape on that canvas, or paint over it entirely!"

Henry throws the brush aside and turns to Michael with wide, dark eyes, and his red lips a little redder from where he always wipes his hand on his mouth as he paints.

"I loved those pups. Do you understand? Do you even know love, my darling?" He studies Michael's face with his slightly mad, lead-addled eyes. "Do you love me?" His face is swollen with tears.

Love? Michael cannot answer that question honestly. Angels aren't incapable of that emotion, but he doesn't feel it for Henry. Not in the way the man feels it for him. So he kisses him, purposely splashing the canvas with paint, covering the treasonous dog-face on the Queen as they fall to the ground, lust easily overcoming Henry's objections.

Asher is still talking. "You're young and you might decide I'm not even worth another screw, or you might think I *am*—and given how you've looked at me all day, I'm hoping at least one more night is absolutely on the table. And if that's all there is, fine. But I'm forty now and I've been too afraid for too long. If I have a chance at something more with you, then I'm going to take it. Everything else be damned. Everything."

"I see."

"I'm sorry. I'm doing this all wrong."

"No, it's not that," Michael says, pulling his cell phone from his pocket and pretending to read a message.

"Do you have to go?"

Michael shakes his head, taps in words and pushes send. Nonsense sent nowhere to no one. "Work. Sorry. What were you saying?"

Asher looks embarrassed. He shakes his head and shrugs. "Nothing. It was nothing."

Seeing Asher retreat when he'd been so brave isn't something he can stomach. "I thought it was damn it all, you want to see if we can have something?"

"Yes."

Michael's grace vibrates so that he trembles all over. "Truth is, I travel a lot. My life isn't my own. I can't make promises or be that kind of person to you."

Asher's visible disappointment slices into Michael's chest and he wants to grab the man, pull him tight, and shelter him under his wings.

"Is it over then?"

"I don't want it to be, but I can't give you what you're asking. So we can end this here, if that's what you want." Every nerve and sinew in his human skin begs for him to give the right response. Michael isn't even sure what right is, but he knows it has to happen now. He holds his breath.

"No. I understand what you're saying. But I want to see you again anyway."

A bell rings somewhere deep in the museum and Michael is swept cold with relief and dread.

"I want to see you again, too."

The hotel room is like an old friend. It pulls Michael in and he drags Asher behind him, mouths latched, clothes coming off, cocks rubbing hard against each other.

Michael knows it's wrong. He's already succeeded in this mission and set Asher on a new path, away from the self-destructive shame and misery that would have ended him. Now Michael is grasping beyond his reach. This isn't what angels are made to do. He should be prostrate before Father, not kneeling at Asher's feet.

He closes his eyes, sucks Asher in, and waits for the punishment to come down on him. Asher moans and clenches his fingers in Michael's hair. His hot whimpers slice through Michael's anxiety and he redoubles his effort, tonguing the slit and working his own hardness with his other hand.

"Thank you," Asher breathes, his head hitting the back of the hotel room door again and again, a soft thump as he struggles to hold back from coming. Michael wants to cradle Asher's head with the back of his hand, but he needs Asher's cock in his throat, and he can't do both at once.

He works his own dick and feels the pressure mounting as Asher gives up and starts to thrust, fucking Michael's face with wild urgency, his cock hitting the back of Michael's throat. The room is filled with the noise of Asher's need and Michael's gurgling grunts.

Michael can feel the orgasm rolling up from his balls and groin. He opens his eyes and stares up at Asher's face, black hair across his forehead, cheeks pink with exertion, and red mouth open wide. If he's going to be cast out for defying Father, for coming back for another taste of this man, then he wants to see everything, feel everything.

He pulls off as Asher starts to come, orgasm pulsing through them both at the same time. Their cries fill the room and Michael feels a burst inside him, the freedom of ecstasy, and he wants it more than almost anything else. He braces himself as the orgasm peaks.

All that falls is their seed onto the carpet.

In the panting aftermath, curled with Asher on the hotel room floor, he stares at the patches of semen, consumed by a strange disappointment.

Four

A week-of-seeing-Asher later, Michael walks five blocks over from Mercy Street to a brand new surf shop on Ocean Drive. The store is small and signage is a big poster with the words, *SURF AND BREAKERS* drawn in gold magic marker. There's also a drawing of a surfboard sporting angel wings, and if he has any doubt he's in the right place, that cinches it.

The chime on the door announces his presence, but it's unnecessary. Lucifer's right there by the counter, grinning like the cocky jerk he is, applying wax to a surfboard. He's tan and his blond hair hangs in long waves not quite to his shoulders. As always, his blue eyes crackle with intelligence and amusement.

"Long time no see, bro."

Michael ignores the slang, though it feels like a hot needle prick, as if Lucifer is flaunting something Michael wants for himself. "It's been a while, brother, yes."

"Let's see, last time I saw you, I was tugging on those annoying white wings of yours trying to pull you out of heaven with me. Good times."

"If you say so." Michael steps closer to the counter, noting that the surfboard is covered in art resembling human tattoos—winged hearts, round-faced birds, and women with large breasts tumbling all over it. His next words are surprisingly true. "A surf shop suits you."

"Doesn't it, bro? Fun, sun, babes, boys, wet, sex. It's all good."

"Why the new shop here?"

Lucifer laughs in his face. "As if you don't know? You called me here, pretty brother. There's rebellion brewing in you and I'm always on board for that, Mike."

"Don't call me 'Mike.'"

"I think it works, actually. When you're cast out, consider switching to it. Michael's so prissy."

Michael ignores the critique of his name and focuses instead on the question that's been plaguing him, the one that lured Lucifer here. "Is it horrible?"

"What?"

"Being cast out. Fallen."

Lucifer grins and wipes a hand over his sweaty forehead. He stops rubbing the wax on his surfboard and takes in the sunset over the ocean, the women walking toward their cars with sand sticking to their flesh, and their skin pink from too much sun.

"Nah. It's all right. Everyone makes being fallen out to be something awful. 'Oh, Father cast him out. He's lost to God's love.'" Lucifer sneers. "How little they know." He waves a hand at Michael and adds, "The old guy's around every day checking in on me."

Michael considers this might be a lie. Lucifer might be trying to trick him. "Every day? If that's true, why doesn't anyone know?"

"He's not shy about it. I guess you idiots up there are so busy laying at his feet that you don't notice if he pops out for an hour or two."

It's disturbing because it's possible. No angel dares look directly at Father.

"Don't you miss it?"

"All that worshiping of his holy highness? Nope. And, if I do say so myself, I think he's kind of proud of me." Lucifer glows a little like the sunset has stroked his skin. "I'm the only one. The only angel who's ever had the guts to really tell him where to shove it."

Michael half expects there to be a rending sound and the room to be torn in two as the wrath of their father smites Lucifer yet again, but nothing happens. If anything, Lucifer looks terrifyingly *free* saying anything he wants without fear of repercussions.

Michael runs his fingers over the corner of the counter, feeling the sharpness of the edge. He doesn't look Lucifer in the eye, when he says, "Do you know about…well, did anyone ever tell you—"

"About that pretty pansy from the bitch queen's court?"

Michael clenches his jaw. "That's no way to—"

"I'm Satan. Cut me some slack."

"Fine. Yes, that's what I was wondering."

"Of course I heard about it." His eyes are alight with glee. "And I know that you're tempted again now. You reek of lust and sex. You're hungry for it. I can practically *taste* it and I've been hard since you walked in."

He gestures at his crotch and Michael sees that, yes, Lucifer's sporting some impressive wood.

"Did *you* put Asher in my path? Did you put Father's stamp on his bones?"

Lucifer cackles. "Not you, too! Do you really think I'd spend time messing with you, Mike, when I can mess with human beings with much more interesting weaknesses?"

Michael isn't sure if he believes him, but, more strikingly, isn't sure he cares. "Father gave me the assignment." Even if Lucifer created the situation, there are other angels, and his father chose *him* to go into this breach.

Lucifer's lips twitch in amusement. "So he sent you into temptation again. Do you really think he's going to deliver you from evil?"

Michael doesn't look at him. Lucifer chuckles. "Oh, I get it now. You don't want him to deliver you, but you can't untangle why he sent you. You still think Father cares. Oh, Mike. It's all a game to him. A test. Will you pass? Will you fail? Will he cast you out or take you in his big, strong, forgiving arms and tell you that it's all right? Tell you that you can go fuck your human friend all you want because he *knows* just how good it feels?"

That is exactly what Michael wants and he feels a flush of embarrassment that Lucifer has read him so well. "I know that will never happen."

"Of course not. Even though he made it feel that way for you. Even though he stamped this Asher with his own holiness and made you want him. He basically made you go back for more."

"Why *me*? Gabriel's good with a human prick and last I checked he hasn't taken a turn in human skins in a decade or more."

"Gabe's a daddy's boy. A total pet. What else would you expect from him? He never has to do the hard stuff. I always did want to punch him in his smug face and—"

"What about Zadkiel? Or Puriel?"

Lucifer waves his hand dismissively. "Zad's always got all that *forgiveness* crap to deal with. He's a busy guy. And would you really set Puriel on a poor human virgin?"

Michael sighs. Of course not. The angel is far too zealous to take his time and not terrify.

"He wasn't called 'pitiless' in the war for nothing. Mike, listen, the old man enjoys this. He's set you up. Just make a choice. I advocate rebellion, of course. It's a lot more satisfying in the end."

Michael feels a tug in his cock and his stomach. He squeezes his eyes shut. Lucifer laughs. "Is it really rebellion if he designed it?"

"Oooooh," Lucifer coos. "You are so close. You've already mostly chosen. But you can't be sure, until you know the worst of it all, right?"

Michael opens his eyes and watches Lucifer rub wax over a drawing of a woman with bulging breasts.

"Let me tell you. The bugger of it is I can't die. So, aside from vacationing down in hell, I'm stuck in human skin forever. It's uncomfortable, as you know. But it has its perks. Sometimes I think I'll just say screw it, tear it off, and let the wings hang out, man. And glow. Just think how I'd glow. And I'd trumpet—because seriously, humans and their Bibles, they love the freaking trumpet—'All who wish to live, bow before me!' And do you know what that would be, Mike?"

Apocalypse. The end of the world.

"What?"

"A really fun day."

Michael can't tell if Lucifer's joking. "He'd end you."

Lucifer shrugs. "He might. He'd be so damn proud. I'm telling you. He likes that I've got some balls."

"What's stopping you?"

"I haven't gotten bored enough yet."

Michael shakes his head. This is the brother he'll have to align himself with if he does this, if he makes this crazy choice. "I have no idea why I thought coming to see you would be helpful."

Lucifer grins, a wicked gleaming thing that makes Michael a little jealous. "Because you knew I'd tell you the truth."

Lucifer goes back to stroking his surfboard and Michael waits long enough that he starts to feel pathetic before he turns to go.

"For what it's worth," Lucifer calls.

Michael stops to listen, but doesn't look back.

"I think he would. Be proud of you, I mean. The old guy loves a good rebellion, and, despite the rap he gets here on earth, he loves sex. He's the one who made it so good, after all."

Michael bangs the door open and barely hears Lucifer yell, "There's always a job for you here, bro. If you need it."

Michael feels sweat prickle his neck as he walks away, the hot sun screaming down at him as the image of himself in a surf shack T-shirt immediately springs to mind. The fact that it's more amusing than unwelcome is troublesome. Maybe he *is* ready to jump ship for an experiment in Lucifer's brand of freedom. Or maybe he's not.

Maybe he'll just meet Asher one last time and be done with it.

For good.

"So, you saw your brother?" Asher asks, panting softly in Michael's arms. His wet, semen-slick cock is shoved against Michael's sticky stomach, and they've barely recovered from their orgasms.

"Yes. He's still an asshole."

"Did you find out what you needed to know?"

He knows Asher doesn't like the cryptic manner in which Michael discusses his work and his family, but Michael can't exactly tell him, "Ash, for the love of your cock and the hot roll of our orgasms, I'm thinking of giving up my eternal gig as the Angel of Justice and Protection and opting to become a cast out, washed up, surf shop employee."

He can't tell him that the idea of walking away from Asher and watching him get involved with someone else, like Henry had all those years ago, makes him want to kick things and maybe start a rebellion that could end with *him* dragging some of his brothers from heaven's grace.

He settles for, "Yes. He can help me if I quit working for my father."

Asher moves on top of Michael, his dick taking interest again, and his eyes hooded. "I can't believe…I mean, we were a one night stand. And now you're quitting your job to be with me? I just came out and it's kind of getting serious really fast." He doesn't seem frightened, though, just pleased. "Maybe I waited so long because you're the—"

Michael cuts him off before he can finish that doomed sentence. "I'm not quitting my job just to be with you."

"You're not?"

"No. I haven't been happy for a long time. A very, very long time. I'm re-evaluating what working for my father costs me, and I've decided it's…" Oh, God, he can't say it. He can't make his mouth form the words.

"Not worth it?"

"It's slavery."

That's something he can say. That's something he knows is true. Submission and absolute obedience aren't doing it for him anymore. He wonders if they're doing it for his father, either. Maybe Lucifer's right. Maybe that's why Father sent him to Asher. Maybe that's why he stamped Asher's bones. Entertainment at Michael's expense isn't beneath him. Being God does gets very tiresome. He knows that.

"That's a little over the top, don't you think?" Asher kisses his lips, nuzzles his neck, and Michael decides that fucking again definitely beats talking about this any longer. Especially when Asher's got his ass on offer this time, dragging Michael's hand down to his hole, whispering, "Finger me. Fuck me," like it's something Asher needs more than air.

Conversation is dropped. Serious focus is applied to open Asher up, and then Michael's shoving his cock in. *So hot, so good.* Nothing beats the pressing simultaneous need to drag this out and surrender to climax.

Asher is so tight, and Michael thinks back to the first time earlier that week, and how Asher had trembled with fear and anticipation, how beautifully he'd spread himself and let Michael inside. They'd both been overcome.

Michael has to wonder, with a spark like theirs, does fucking ever get old? So far, the only thing that has stopped them is their human bodies' reluctance to perform an unlimited number of times, and Asher's sense of self-preservation. If Michael had his druthers, they'd simply never quit—not for food, not for drink, not for anything. Not even for Father. He supposes that's why it's wrong, and why he'll be cast out.

Asher's on his stomach letting loose with loud, hoarse cries as

Michael fucks him. Banging on the wall from the hotel room next door leaves Asher trying to cover his sounds of pleasure by biting into the pillow. Michael holds back his own groans, pressure rising inside as he denies himself that vent. Asher spasms beneath him, his ass clenching rhythmically around Michael's cock, and the scent of semen fills the air. Asher's orgasm ricochets in Michael when he pushes into his flesh and bones, taking in his pleasure, and pulsing his grace to extend it.

Michael licks his lips, closes his eyes, and fucks him harder. Asher's legs skid all over the bed, his hands grip the pillow and clench white-knuckled hard, but he yells for Michael to keep going, *don't stop*, so he doesn't.

Pounding into Asher's convulsing ass, ignoring the thump-thump-thump of the person on the other side of the wall as Asher's cries can't be contained, Michael succumbs to it—a rip of pleasure that obliterates him. He screams as he loses control, his human form unable to contain his ecstasy, and as he pushes deep into Asher's trembling body, he breaks free—wings unfurling and spreading wide. He arches back, and comes, and comes, and comes.

Holding Asher still beneath him with the weight of his body, hoping he doesn't open his scrunched eyes or roll over to witness the spread of Michael's wings, Michael folds them back into scapulae. Sweat-drenched and still throbbing, he takes inventory: he's smiling, he's humming, he's happy. He's not fallen yet.

Asher laughs and shoves out from under Michael before turning around to grab him around the waist. "You think your brother might have a job for me, too?" Asher grins up at him.

"Probably," Michael says, though he isn't sure letting Asher around Lucifer is a good idea. It isn't as if it would be out of character for Lucifer to decide that Michael's lover would be a delightful plaything. "But I'm not sure working together is a great idea."

"True. I've got some applications in," Asher says. "I'm hoping one pays off soon, because I'd like to get my own place. Living with my folks isn't going to cut it if this," he gestures between them, "is going to be anything. And we can't keep meeting in a hotel, can we?"

Michael has never considered the entire living situation aspect. He wonders if he would require a job or if his divinely given abilities to influence people to do anything he wants will remain intact after...well, if he chooses something he probably won't choose. The real danger is of Father deciding to simply cast him out for the choices he's daring to make. Before that happens he should understand more of what might lie ahead. He'll ask Lucifer about those details soon. Until then, he can easily maneuver himself into a house if he wants, and Asher can live there. His absences might cause a lot of questions, which he can probably cover up as travel for Father's job. Though the idea of future sexual assignments seems unsavory now.

Are more lies really the way to start your new life, Mike? He hears Lucifer's voice in his head and he rolls his eyes. This is complicated stuff and Lucifer loves complicated. Though he doubts Lucifer's ever felt the warm, happy sensation engulfing him in waves every time he lays eyes on Asher. He's not going to give that feeling a name. If he doesn't say it, then it isn't true, and he can pretend what he has with Asher is something he'll eventually get tired of.

Except in every single way it isn't, for reasons Michael still can't really put into words.

He knows it's often like this for humans. They can meet thousands of people in their lives before coming across one who sparks a connection they don't want to live without. He listens fondly as Asher continues talking, realizing he could listen for hours and be utterly content.

"Job hunting is the pits. Talk about new lessons in failure and ego-crushing rejection."

Michael touches Asher and infuses him with all the rosy, warm feeling in him. Asher reddens and glances down, pleased at the understanding that passes between them.

"At least I know you don't see me that way," he says.

"I never have and I never will." Michael carries on before he acts on the affection he can feel vibrating in Asher's flesh and bones, echoed in his own human form, and ringing throughout his angelic one, too. "Where are you hoping to hear back from most?"

"Synagogue," Asher says, his dark eyes sparkling. "They need a new bookkeeper and since I did that for Dad awhile, I thought why not?"

Synagogue. Of course. Michael almost laughs. Well, at least he knows exactly how to make that happen for Asher—a visit to the rabbi, which the man will soon thereafter forget, and it's a done deal. The pay will probably be slightly more than Asher is expecting as well. All the better for moving out of his parents' home.

Michael's insides quiver at the thought of using his powers for something *he* wants for a change. He wonders if this is how Lucifer feels all the time, or if after thousands of years he's accustomed to the sensation of freedom now.

"I've been thinking," Asher says, as he turns on his side and reaches out to thumb the small indent in Michael's chin. "I want to know more about you, about your family. I know it's early for this, but, maybe I could meet your dad?"

"Meet my…? Well, he's hard to pin down."

"Your mother? You've never mentioned her."

"Entirely out of the picture. It's almost like she never existed."

Asher frowns. "I'm sorry. That must have been hard growing up. My mom and I are close—or we used to be before I realized what I was. I can't imagine my life without her in it."

"Tell me about her," Michael says, meaning it earnestly. He suddenly wants to know every last detail of Asher's mother. He can breathe in and catch the imprint of Asher's childhood still lingering around him, and it's warm, glowing, like the happy dreams of humans he's sometimes looked in on.

"Well, her name's Marie and she's almost seventy now. She's retired. She used to work for the phone company when I was in high school, but when I was a little kid, she stayed home. Some of my favorite memories were of her greeting me when I came in the door after school. She always seemed so genuinely happy to see me then."

"Not now?"

"Oh, sure. I guess. It's hard to say. I mean, I'm a pretty big disappointment to her. No job, no wife, probably gay." He looks at Michael. "Definitely gay. Actually, I was going to tell you, but we…got distracted." He blushes prettily. "Anyway, I told her last night and my father, too."

Michael's skin prickles and he stifles the nearly overwhelming urge to stretch his wings again and shelter Asher under them. "Are you okay?"

He lets himself see into Asher's body, reading his bones and flesh, and he knows the answer isn't as bad as it could be.

"My father told me he didn't want to hear that kind of bullshit and left the room."

"I'm sorry."

"My mother said she'd known it for a long time but had hoped it wasn't true." Asher frowns and fiddles with the edge of a sheet. "Her brother is gay and she says she recognized some of the signs in me."

Michael stops his hand and twines their fingers together. Asher meets Michael's eyes and relaxes. "And then?" Michael asks because he knows that's not all of it. He can feel the rest of it bubbling in Asher, a mixture of pain, hope, and determination.

"We didn't talk about it again until dinner. My mother told my father she expects him to accept me and he didn't say he wouldn't."

"It's a start."

"I always thought he'd hurt me—kill me even."

Michael thinks of Lucifer's face as he fell—proud, surprised, and angry. He sees a touch of that in Asher's eyes and feels an echoing call of it in his own chest.

Asher's hand squeezes in his. "What about you? Have you told your parents?"

"My father knows, and like I said, my mother isn't in my life."

"How did he take it?"

"He understands. He's supportive." There's really no good way to say 'he sent me to you' because that makes Father sound rather like a pimp. And, hey, well, now that he's considered it… Michael chuckles at the thought.

"Wow, it's a different world today. You kids have it so easy."

Michael scoffs. "I've told you, I'm not a kid."

Asher rolls his eyes and pulls away, flopping onto his back to stare at the ceiling. Michael feels dissatisfaction well up inside him. That's not how he wants Asher to react at all. He wants to see him smile again.

"When I was growing up, there wasn't any hope for someone like me. Or if there was, it was only just starting to be a glimmer on the horizon and you had to move to San Francisco or New York City. You couldn't live here."

"Los Angeles is just down the road. Why didn't you move?"

"Because I have obligations to my family and because I'm not the kind of guy who does that kind of thing. I'm a coward, Michael. In case you didn't notice."

Michael breathes in and out slowly, feeling the power folded into his wings. He used to lead armies into war. He defeated Lucifer and his father called him The Archangel, and he'd been proud. Tired, but proud. Once, Michael had been glorious. Now what is he?

"I'd be satisfied with meeting your brother," Asher says, coming back to the original topic.

Michael knows he's referring to Lucifer but chooses to obfuscate by asking, "Which one?"

"Any of them?"

"None of them are worth meeting, I promise."

"Michael, the cryptic refusal to reveal anything about yourself has to stop. How many brothers do you have?"

"Four," he says. The lie tastes bad in his mouth. He forges ahead. "Zad, Rafe, Luke, and Gabe."

"And you don't remember your mother?"

"I'm the youngest. She was gone before my memories begin."

Another lie. Can this feeling keep growing between them if there are always so many lies?

Oh, bro, now you're worried about the feelings? Love! Ain't it the grandest? You're screwed.

"And your father runs this big business. Did he inherit it, or build it himself?"

"Oh, he built it himself. From scratch."

From nothing into everything, Father spoke it into being.

"I know you've said it's complicated, but it can't have always been. Tell me about how he got started."

Michael remembers a time when mankind was a small experiment his father was running. How quickly that experiment blossomed into a cottage industry! Back then it was easy to be an angel. He showed up with his hair aflame, and the people cowered before him and feared to lift their eyes to his countenance.

Then there was the Great War and things changed. The whole Jesus situation had led to some complicated interactions, too, and Mohammed confused it all over again.

Now that little cottage industry has morphed into something akin to the largest corporation imaginable. A rather poorly managed one, at that, if he dares say so himself. Father doesn't seem to mind the mess his creations live in. If anything, he's having fun watching his wind-up toys run, throwing more cogs in the works and laughing when the people blame Lucifer.

Well, he supposes Father laughs about that. Come to think of it, he's never really heard Father laugh. He wonders if he can and what it might sound like.

"Well?" Asher prompted. "Your father's business?"

"It's a dull story. Have you read Genesis?"

"Yes, of course."

"Did you read all of it?"

"Well, no. I stopped when I got to the begats, but what does that have to do with anything? Sometimes I feel like you got a degree in double speak in college."

"Alas, if only I'd known they offered that major," Michael teases. "The story of my father's business is much the same—in the beginning there was my Father and he was lonely."

"With five sons he was lonely?"

"I thought you wanted to hear about his business?"

"I do!"

"Then, yes, he was lonely even with his five sons and all of my many cousins." Michael feels better now that he's at least acknowledged the rest of his brethren. "And he was bored."

"With five boys he was bored? I'm surprised he had time to even think."

"Oh, all the time in the world. So in his boredom, he made a thing or two, and then made a few more things, and that led to even more things."

"What are these things?"

"All kinds of things. It's hard to begin to encompass the extent of it."

"Try."

"Well, let's put it this way, eventually his creations made their way all over the earth and, if you ask me, they'll eventually play a role in destroying it."

"So your father created the Cylons from *Battlestar Galactica*?" Asher says. His amusement is touched with annoyance.

"Very much like that, actually. You'd be surprised."

Asher laughs and shakes his head. "I wish you'd be honest with me, Michael."

Michael wishes he could, too. "I'm being honest, just not forthright. Believe me, I made it all sound much more interesting than it really is."

Asher sighs and runs a hand over his chest, wiping away come and sweat.

"I'll tell you what," Michael says, the compromise on his tongue the very instant it forms in his head. "Meeting my father is out of the question at the moment, but how about I agree to meet yours?"

Asher goes pale and his breathing goes still. "You really want to do that?"

What are you doing, bro? This right here? This is stupid.

"I do," Michael says.

FIVE

Asher's mother is petite and smells of caramel when she opens the door of the house. Michael had carefully considered his offering before arriving and he extends the small, potted and beribboned hydrangea to her. Michael pushes it gently into her hands and sees that she knows the meaning of a hydrangea given as a gift. *Grateful for the recipient's understanding.*

"How lovely!" she says, taking it from him. "Thank you, dear."

"You're welcome, Mrs.—"

"Call me Marie."

"Michael," he says and she smiles at him.

"Come in, come in."

She puts the hydrangea on the entryway table, centering it just so, then turns and takes his light jacket. She hangs it up on the neat coatrack by the door.

Michael spots Asher's tennis shoes at the base of it, the strings unlaced and dangling. Warmth rises in him and his cheeks burn, his heart tripping.

He's momentarily baffled by the emotion—the shoes are just shoes. Asher is just a human. Yet there is something about him—his vulnerability, his determination, his specific way of tilting his head, the sound he makes when he's surprised—so many tiny particulars that add up to a person Michael is unwilling to walk away from. It isn't just Father's stamp. He refuses to believe it's only that.

"My, you are such a handsome young man," Marie says, as he follows her down the hallway.

Michael's cheating, he knows. He's turned the angelic light up a little and there's no way Marie will be able to resist that. Asher's father is a tougher nut to crack, as evidenced by his frown and refusal to rise from his recliner when Michael walks into the room.

"Gay and a cradle robber," he mutters after a fast flick of the eye toward Michael. "This is the thanks we get."

"Michael," Asher says from the kitchen doorway, dishtowel on his shoulder, and his dark hair tousled. He has a dark spot of something brown and gooey near the collar of his red shirt. "I'm glad you're here. Come in the kitchen."

Marie kicks Asher's father's shoe. As Michael moves toward the kitchen, he hears her whisper loudly, "Ira, have some manners. Do not embarrass me in my home."

Asher's smile is tight as he pulls Michael into the warm kitchen. "Sorry about my dad." Then he frowns, a deep, sudden expression of concern that makes Michael's stomach hurt.

"I want you to feel comfortable here and he's ruining it."

"I'm fine. He's fine, too."

Relief sweeps over Asher's face, echoing Michael's feelings.

Michael drops onto the bar stool at the counter when Asher waves a hand toward it. There's a mess of wax paper and apples and a bowl of brown goo set out there.

"Mom made shepherd's pie for dinner. Meanwhile, I was making kosher caramel apples for her to take to synagogue for the children's program tomorrow."

"Buttering up your potential new boss through your mother?"

"Every little bit helps. I'm just really grateful he's even considering me for the position." Asher's cheeks flush a little and he clears his throat.

Michael's eyebrow lifts of its own accord. "Is the rabbi considering you for another position I should be aware of?"

A dark chasm opens in him, one he's never known before. He's risking so much, perhaps foolishly, for this. What if Asher doesn't return the same level of affection and loyalty? Humans often don't.

Asher meets his eye with a twinkle and a blush. "He's married and straight." He stabs an apple through with a cooking skewer and dunks it into the caramel. "Attractive, yes, but competition? No."

The darkness in Michael recedes, but he still senses a dark spot of it, like a stain. He clears his throat.

"Why? Would you have been jealous?" Asher asks, nonchalantly.

"Of course."

He's said the right thing. Asher's eyes light up and he leans over the counter to press a fast kiss to Michael's cheek.

"Now, now, I just got your father settled. None of that or you'll get him riled up again." Marie takes up a place beside Asher and together the three of them make caramel apples and talk about Michael.

It's horribly easy to lie. He's very good at it. Lies of omission and other outright misrepresentations are a staple of his job. It just feels wrong now when it's Asher he's lying to.

"So, you've traveled the world," Marie says, carefully putting one of the last apples down on the wax paper. "Working for your father selling mysterious items—"

"Not so mysterious," Michael says. "More ephemeral."

"So, finances then. You're in finances."

He laughs. "It's so much worse than finances, Mrs. Rosenthal."

"Crime. You're a mobster."

Michael sits up straight and nods his head. "You've found me out. I'm absolutely a mobster."

"As if," Asher murmurs, and quickly amends, "Well, if mobsters are angels, maybe."

Michael's heart does a strange tap dance. But a quick look into Asher reveals that he's only teasing in an affectionate and loving way. He hasn't guessed. He doesn't know.

But would it be such a bad thing if Asher did know? How can Michael ever tell him?

"Your son is right. I'm much too angelic to be a mobster."

"Though, your innocent face would be the perfect cover," Asher says, thoughtfully. "I know, let me guess—you're a spy."

Michael laughs. An argument could be made that he *is* a spy of sorts.

"Oh, my, aren't you two cute together. I never thought I'd see this day," Marie says. "And it's nice."

"I'm happy to hear that, ma'am."

Marie goes back to focusing on Michael's career aspirations. "Well, Asher says you may be leaving your father's employ soon?"

"Yes, I'm considering working for my brother. He owns a surf shop."

"Quite a step down," she tuts.

"Yes, quite a steep tumble actually."

He can't believe he's joking about it and he should use his angelic power to wipe their minds of questions, but he can't do that to Asher. Not now. So he just shakes his head and says, "Mrs. Rosenthal, how can I help with dinner?"

Marie turns to the cupboard and pulls out plates, amusement and happiness shining in her eyes as she hands them to Michael and indicates the table.

Michael smiles when Asher washes his hands and pulls silverware from a drawer. Their bodies brush as they lay the places together and each touch is a tingling reminder of why he's here and why he's risking it all.

Dinner is tense with Ira saying barely a word, but when it's over Asher's father stands up, puts his hands on his hips, and sticks his bulging stomach out. "I didn't expect to raise a queer, but since I have, I'll accept my lot. If you come around a few more times, I'll consider learning your name. Until then, you're on probation. I want to see how long you actually stay in my son's life."

"I understand, sir," Michael murmurs as Ira leaves the room and heads back to his recliner.

"He's having a hard time," Marie says, smiling sadly. "But everything passes, and this will, too."

"Hopefully before he does," Asher mutters.

Michael puts out his hand and takes Asher's fingers. He's saying the words before he can really think about them and when he hears them come out of his mouth, he only feels a thrill of excitement. "I want to be here when he gets over it."

"Well," Marie says, standing up to clear dishes. "You're suggesting a very big commitment, since that's likely to take years."

Asher grins and squeezes Michael's fingers. "I'm okay with years."

"Me, too."

"Dude, how does it not even occur to you that this is what he wants you to do?" Lucifer says, slamming his empty beer mug down and motioning for another. The bar is crowded with people, and everyone's jostling for the bartender's attention, but of course he serves Lucifer first.

"He wants me to fall?"

"He sets you up with this guy—which, bro, seriously, could you look more lovesick?—and then leaves you to twist over whether or not you want to keep on serving the whims of His Divinely Fickle Highness or bravely step into the new world order, embracing love and sex and human skin."

Lucifer glows as he warms to his speech. His blond hair shines with an unearthly glow in the low light. Women take notice, and a few men, too. Lucifer does nothing to conceal it.

"And he hasn't given you any assignments since, now has he? Why's that?" He pounds his palm against the wood of the bar. "Because this one isn't over, bro. That's all there is to it. He's planned this and now you get to act it out for him. A puppet in his play."

Michael searches himself. This doesn't feel like something he's acting out on behalf of Father. He remembers Asher's profile that morning, outlined by the light from the hotel window as he put on his socks. His nose standing out, backlit, and beautiful. He remembers the strange roll in his stomach when Asher laughs, or the aching fondness he feels when he catches Asher looking at himself in the mirror, touching the small wrinkles by his eye. He loves those wrinkles and feels squishy inside whenever Asher smiles enough for them to pop out.

Every other assignment he's ever been sent on, even Henry, and even as the leader of the Great War for Heaven, has felt like more of a strain than this attachment to Asher and his particulars. He doesn't even have to reach for it. Not even a little bit.

"Ah, man, look at you, bro. It's a sad day when you look that lost."

"I'm not lost."

"Yet."

"Touché."

The song on the jukebox in the corner comes to a jangling close and Lucifer turns to it, points a finger, and within a few moments a beachy, summery song with female vocals fills the room. The chorus comes quickly and Lucifer sings it at Michael with fake cow-eyes of love. "*Falling, falling,*" the women sing over and over. "I'm falling, falling," Lucifer sings along with them.

Michael's phone buzzes and he pulls it from his pocket. It's Asher, of course, texting with a picture of his mother in the garden, digging out a place for the new hydrangea Michael brought her. She's small and looks fragile, but Michael knows she's full of secret strength. The phone buzzes again and this time it's a selfie of Asher's grinning face with a thumbs-up held next to his cheek, his mom's hunched form barely visible in the background. Michael smiles to see Asher's cheesy smile, so fake and ridiculous, and yet his eyes are bright with real joy.

Another buzz.

My mother says you are a charming young man and very beautiful. My father glared at her. I think you're amazing.

"Aw, look at your widdle face! Damn, Mike, I haven't seen you look that genuinely happy in, fuck…forever, man. You've *never* looked like that. Not when you were Father's favorite, not when you were kicking the shit out of me in the war, not when you pried my hot hands off your wings and sent me tumbling." Lucifer makes a grab at the phone. "I'm telling you, he's doing this to you on purpose, and you should just fall right into it. I'll make sure you have a soft landing." He captures the phone from Michael and looks at the picture of Asher and laughs harder. "Or, hell, *he* will. Look at him. You always had a thing for the Jews."

Michael doesn't try to grab his phone back. He's not going to fall into some ridiculous physical fight with Lucifer in this place. He waits until Lucifer's flipped through the other photos Asher has sent in the last few weeks of their relationship.

"Lover Boy with kitty cat. Lover Boy giving a seductive smile—did that get you hard, Mike? I bet it got you hard. Hmm, Lover Boy sends a lot of pictures of flowers. Wait, I see, there's a pattern here. Clover and a note for good luck for your meeting with your dad, ha, and coreopsis for joy with the message—'so happy I met you.' Oh, sick, bro. He's sending you love notes and flower pics to match. That's not normal, dude. That's like some kind of faggy crap," Lucifer says with a serious expression, and then bursts into a radiant grin, singing under his breath, "Falling, falling!"

As he hands the phone back to Michael, he changes the lyrics of the first part of the next verse from something innocuous and cliché to, "There ain't no love like an anal love, and two dicks are better than one!"

"You're as annoying as ever."

"And you lack a sense of humor. Shocking! Does this guy make you laugh, 'cause Baby Jesus, you need to laugh."

"Must you reference him? Whatever. You know, why do I keep coming to you for advice? You have nothing to offer me."

"I've offered you the best advice you're gonna get, Mike. Let go. Feel the gravity. Taste the dirt when you hit the ground. It's not all that bad and you'll like it. I promise."

"Oh, *Eve*, that knowledge you're holding there in your sweet innocent hand will taste so very good and won't hurt you at all! I promise!"

"She liked it." Lucifer looks pleased with himself.

"She did," Michael agrees. "And he did, too."

Singing again, but not necessarily along with the song, which has now changed to something else, Lucifer opines, "Once you got it, you can't let it go, you gotta have it, bro. So just give in!"

"Keep your day job," Michael says.

"Hey, I did the rock star gig, if you recall. I was crazy successful at it."

"Yeah, after the actor gig, and the politician gig. Which, by the way, seemed to be your best. It certainly produced the most evil results."

"Yeah, but I'm not *all* bad, you know. I mean, I don't really want only evil shit to happen. It's just a little more fun when it does."

Michael chuckles softly, taking a sip of his beer.

"*There* you go, brother. Laugh a little. When's the last time you had fun?"

He thinks about Asher's mouth on his cock the night before. It'd been a sweet encounter, both of them feeling very skin-hungry. They'd held hands while Asher bobbed his head up and down, saliva running down to Michael's balls. Asher's little sounds as he'd worked had been so sweet and urgent, and when Michael orgasmed—wings pushing against his skin, aching there angrily—Asher had swallowed it all, gripping Michael's fingers and nursing his cockhead for every drop.

Heat pools in Michael's groin and he swallows another mouthful, lust surging in him, along with that weird ache that only eases when he's near Asher, and is, otherwise, a rotten pain in his neck. Is this what humans know as love? Romantic love? It's so much more visceral than the heavenly stuff.

Lucifer's still talking. "Rock star was fun, too, not quite as easy to really get in there and fuck shit up, but whatever. I figure resting a few years in a surf shop, taking sweet jaunts off to commit hardcore mischief when necessary, should put the bite back into my badness soon enough." He claps Michael on the back. "And it looks like I might have someone to leave the shop to when I go."

Michael ignores that and asks, "Is it fun being bad?"

"Nah, it's mostly boring because it's so easy. It's kind of pathetic. You know, you'd think if he was going to make them, he'd have made them a little less simple."

"Simple." He thinks of Asher's smile and his mother's watchful gaze over dinner the night before. He thinks of Asher's father's tight mouth. "Right."

"So, recently, I've been thinking I should spend a little more time messing with the Christians. Such a dramatic lot, those kids."

Michael shakes his head and glances over his shoulder at the exit. He's only a ten minute walk from the hotel. Asher is going to be there soon, and he suddenly wants nothing more than to go there and wait for him.

Lucifer raises his beer and clangs it against Michael's sitting on the bar. He takes a long swig and wipes his lips with the back of his hand. "The real question, Mike? Is why he never just blows that damn horn or sends in the messiah. Did you ever ask yourself about that?"

He has actually, many times. But he's never been daring enough to ask Father. Maybe, one day, if he's ever sure that he wants twenty years with Asher more than he wants forever as his father's tool, he'll come out and demand a response.

"I'm not sure he's got a plan."

Lucifer's eyebrows go up. "Whoa, blasphemy, bro."

"I mean, *surely* he's got a plan? Right?"

Lucifer just stands up and pats him on the shoulder. "Whatever you need to tell yourself."

"Wait," Michael grabs his wrist.

"Yes?"

"It's just…why him?"

"Why who?"

Michael grips him hard, showing him a little of his strength. He may have lost the taste for it, and he may be out of practice, but he is still a warrior.

"Why Lover Boy?"

"Why him in particular? He's not special." Yet as soon as the words are out, he wants to argue with himself about the pure specialness of Asher's smile.

Michael sighs as Lucifer sits down again and slaps the bar with both hands. "There's the rub. Why anyone? Love is a mystery and why any human falls for another is something I can never understand." Lucifer lifts a brow. "But you're not human are you? And since I've never done the deed myself—fallen in love, I mean—I can't say what it's all about. It happens. It sometimes sticks and sometimes doesn't. People make stupid choices for it." He sneers. "Case in point."

"I don't know why I ask you things."

"Me either. Stop analyzing it and just let yourself love the human. You want to, and what's the worst that can happen?" Lucifer points at the jukebox and the song about falling starts up again. "Bye, bro. You're gonna have to figure it out on your own. I've got some badness to get into."

"If you must."

Lucifer stands up. "I'll see you Monday."

"What's on Monday?"

"Your first day of work at the surf shop. Every fallen angel needs to work, now doesn't he?" Lucifer winks, ruffles Michael's hair affectionately, and walks out singing under his breath about anal love.

"Great." Sunlight breaks into the room and vanishes again with the swing of the door. "Because I'd hate to be unemployed." He looks down at Asher's picture on the phone again and his heart flips. "Someone in this relationship needs a job."

SIX

And a place to live.

The house isn't huge but it's large enough to give them both space and in the master bedroom there's a large bathtub in which Michael can soak to offset the pain of keeping his wings tucked in. The backyard is a nice mix of sun and shade that will support a garden for Asher to fill with his choice of flowers, shrubs, and vegetables.

Asher loves the house. At least he seems to based on his enthusiastic texts in response to the photos Michael has sent him of each room.

Are you sure? This is so impulsive! Asher replies when Michael says he's arranged for the purchase.

Impulsive is my middle name.

Michael stares at the teasing words he shot back, high on Asher's happiness, and buzzing with a giddy sensation that he's never experienced before. This house is *his* and the choices he makes in it are his, as well. A life apart from duty and servitude. Rebellion.

It feels so big it might crush him.

It feels amazing.

He's going to make a life with Asher. He has no idea what he'll tell Father when he finally calls him to duty again. What he'll do. Go, he supposes. And come home to Asher. This house, this plot of land in the country. Perhaps one day he'll even be able to spread his wings here and show Asher who he truly is.

Will Asher love him anyway? He believes the answer is yes, or else he wouldn't be here with this key in his hand and the deed to this property in his pocket.

Michael stands on the back porch staring at the roll of green land extending to a bank of trees, imagining the flowerbeds Asher will put in. Near the back of the property they can plant daffodil bulbs to represent a new beginning for both of them. He smiles cynically as the double meaning of the narcissus comes to mind.

Is this what selfishness feels like?

No wonder his brother enjoys it so much.

He waits for Father's retribution for his rebellious thoughts and deeds, but nothing happens. Michael wonders what he's waiting for, what action will take it far enough that his father forces him to choose, or simply casts him out. Whatever the line is, he hasn't crossed it yet.

That night, holding Asher close against him on the brand new mattress they've just broken in, he kisses the shell of Asher's ear and whispers, "I love you."

A warm delight spikes and Michael opens himself up to let Asher feel it.

"I love you, too."

"Tomorrow do you want to go looking at furniture?" He can have the place decorated with a snap of his fingers, but he wants Asher to help him choose. It seems like something human lovers do.

"Sure, that'd be fun." There's hesitancy in his voice and Michael wants to smooth it away.

"But what?"

"I've been thinking." Asher turns on his side to look at Michael earnestly. "What do you see in me? You're so young and beautiful. You could have anyone at all."

"I see all the particulars of you that make you Asher, and I love them," Michael says, reaching out to brush Asher's dark hair from his shining forehead. "This kind of spark comes once or twice in a hundred years. Trust me."

Asher rolls his eyes and laughs. "Yes, if you say so, oh, ye wildly experienced child."

"I'm not a child, Asher." He sounds petulant but that's only because he knows he has to be honest with Asher sooner rather than later. If Lucifer is telling the truth, he won't die, though Asher will. Eventually there'll be no denying his inhumanness, and explanations will have to be given. If he waits too long there will be no hope. A shiver passes through him at the thought that in Asher's reaction to the truth lies the dénouement of the relationship.

"Are you cold?" Asher pulls him closer, sweaty skin on sweaty skin.

"Keep me warm."

"I will," Asher says. "I've been thinking of other things, too."

"Like?"

"That you can't keep blocking me out of your life. I deserve to know where you work and what you really do when you're not with me."

Michael swallows thickly, his grace pressing against his skin, aching to wipe hard questions from Asher's mind. But what would that make him then? It is one thing to use his powers for Father's work, but for his own ends? That's Lucifer's territory. "I know. You're right."

Asher blinks at him and sighs. "I've also been thinking about that night you picked me up. You did it to protect me, didn't you? Like your namesake, the archangel Michael. You swooped in and saved me, huh?"

Michael starts to say he did it because he finds Asher unbearably attractive, but takes another tack. "What did I save you from?"

"From making the mistake of going home with that other guy."

Michael nods slowly. "I didn't see that turning out well."

"How do you know?"

Michael shrugs. "He wouldn't have been gentle." Asher tilts his head and narrows his eyes skeptically. "He was the type to hurt you whether he meant to or not."

"You know what I think? I think that night you needed me just as much as I needed you." Asher grins, kisses Michael's lips. "You needed someone to love. Get you out of your mid-twenties rut. Make you choose yourself over what your dad wants for the first time in your life."

"Maybe that's so."

"I have a question for you to ponder," Asher says, as he gets up from the mattress, turns on the new space heater set up by the window, and then heads toward the bathroom.

"Okay."

He pauses in the doorway, smiles cheekily, all sweet, flushed face, and glittering black eyes. "If that's true, who really saved who here?"

Michael feels an odd tightness in his chest, a thickness in his throat. Is that wetness in his eyes? Are these tears? Is he so happy he's going to cry? "My hero," he whispers. "My savior."

Asher laughs as he turns away.

"Wait." His chest aches, his wings burn against his back. "It's time that I'm honest with you."

"Should I be worried?"

Michael nods and Asher's vibrant eyes shutter. This shivery burst in his body is new and Michael recognizes it as anxiety. He's experienced dread and fear of Father before, but never of a human being. Asher has more power than he knows.

Michael takes comfort in the fact that Asher only puts on his boxer shorts and slides his burgundy button-up shirt on over his shoulders before sitting on the edge of the mattress. It implies a trust that Michael might not deserve but hopes to benefit from anyway.

The space heater whirs and Michael twists his fingers together.

"I'm listening," Asher whispers, sliding his hand forward across the mattress toward him, palm up.

But Michael doesn't take the offered comfort. Instead he stands, naked and vulnerable. Asher gazes up at him with soft, worried eyes, the creases by his mouth deepening into a frown.

"Just tell me. Whatever it is, I'll be okay."

Michael reaches out to heaven, feeling the connection at his back, and he waits to see what Father will do. Will he stop him now?

His wings unfurl with a crisp snap, always eager to be free of human skin, stretching to touch the walls on either side of the room. Michael tamps back his bursting radiance to avoid blinding Asher with his angelic grace.

Words are unnecessary.

Blood drains from Asher's cheeks and he goes completely still. No fight or flight in him—no breath even—frozen in awe before the archangel of heaven. As he should be.

Asher's eyes are wide, his jaw dropped, and when Michael pushes into Asher's bones he finds only terror. Without speaking or reaching out, he allows the moment to drag on and take up space in the eternity he lives in and which far exceeds Asher's imagining.

Air rushes into Asher's lungs with a rattle and he scrambles to his feet and back until he's pressed against the wall, hyperventilating and shaking. A shrill keen pierces the air, pushed out of him between shuddering breaths.

"Peace," Michael says and pushes it into Asher's flesh, willing it into him.

Asher melts to the floor, weak-limbed and still trembling, but the keening stops, replaced with rasping, slowing breaths.

"I mean you no harm."

Asher turns green and Michael sends him a wave of strength and another push of peace.

"What—you—what's happening? This isn't real." Asher's voice is slow, like he's piecing the words together from a tangle of thoughts. Michael can know these thoughts, can read his mind like he did the first night in the bar, but there's a certain respect that comes with being someone's lover and not their guardian angel. Asher deserves his privacy.

"It is real. I am Michael."

"The Archangel. That's absurd." He runs his hand over his face and stares desperately at Michael's wings. "This is a dream. I'll wake up soon."

Michael steps forward and Asher screams, pressing himself back against the wall, arm up, like a child shielding himself from a parent's raised switch.

"I won't hurt you." Michael reaches out but doesn't touch. "I love you."

Asher stares at him.

"The night we met my father sent me to teach you self-acceptance, to show you his love."

Asher blinks rapidly. "Please stop."

"Would you feel more comfortable if I folded my wings beneath my skin again?" The incandescent fear that he's enjoyed in many a mortal upon his revelation isn't enjoyable at all on Asher.

"If you *what*?"

Michael flexes, carefully tucking the primaries into the upper wing coverts, and sighs as his skin smooths into place.

Asher leans over and vomits.

"It's overwhelming to be in the presence of an angel," Michael says in his most gentle tones. "Allow me to soothe you. I have the ability to reduce your fear."

Asher wipes his mouth with the back of his hand, the stench of vomit rising around them. Michael snaps his fingers and whisks it away.

"How did you…?" Asher's voice trembles. "What do you want from me?"

To be your boyfriend seems an absurd response but it's the only true one. Still Michael says nothing for a moment, trying to formulate a comprehensive answer.

"Am I dead?"

"No. You're very much alive. This is very real. And I am breaking many rules by being here now with you."

"Breaking rules?" Asher looks around with fear screaming through him, echoing in the room as it radiates from his flesh.

"Angels don't fall in love."

"Fall in love." Asher is stuck and Michael has to reach into him, permission or no, to free him so he can understand.

"This won't hurt," Michael says, feeling his way through Asher's body, suffusing him with true peace. He guides Asher's heartbeat and breath until his eyes are no longer sharp and wild, until he's rubbing at his face and looking warily at Michael, but no longer insensible with fear. "Asher Rosenthal, I am the Archangel and I'm at your service."

Surely this is the sacrilege that will bring Father's wrath. But he still feels his link home like a golden thread at his back and there's no hint of a disturbance from heaven.

"You came for me," Asher whispers. "After all these years."

"Father has a strange sense of timing." And a comedic one at that, if Lucifer is to be believed.

Asher leans his head back against the wall and stares up at Michael. "What does this mean?"

"It means I'm even more angelic than you already believed me to be."

It's too early for jokes. Asher doesn't laugh.

"It means I love you and you needed to know the truth." Michael smiles ruefully, stretching his shoulders that already ache from the wings. "I couldn't let you move your things in without understanding who you're living with."

"What I'm living with," Asher says, his voice low enough that it's more breath than sound.

"Allow me to explain who I am." Michael sits on the floor across from Asher, folding his legs like a pretzel and starting at a point in time that is vaguely the beginning and leaving out eons to get to the point where they are now.

By the time he's done talking, Asher's eyes are wide again and he compulsively wipes his hand over his mouth over and over, like he's pushing away words he's afraid to speak.

"You can say anything," Michael says. "I know you have questions."

"Why?"

There's all of time in that question, the weight of him, the wear. But the truth's not an answer Asher can ever comprehend. "Because of these," he says, touching the wrinkles fanning from the edges of Asher's eyes. "And because you're right. You did save me that night. I'd never felt a pull for any other human the way I did for you. Did Father put you in my path to fall in love with you? I don't know. But I have. I did. I can't say why. I've met so many humans, but you're different for me." Michael struggles to explain himself and his feelings. Do humans have to justify their love? "You're my savior, my hero."

The back of his neck prickles ominously. He's close now.

"More like your damnation," Asher says, shaking his head.

"Not as you understand it." Michael struggles for words to explain. He takes Asher's hand. "A fallen angel is barred from heaven and no longer feels Father's presence fully." He adds quietly, "Lucifer claims Father comes to visit him. He claims Father is proud of him even now."

"Lucif—you mean, Luke? Your brother at the surf shop? He's Satan?"

Michael makes a face. "Yes."

Asher huffs out a shocked laugh, mouth working before asking incredulously, "Is that why you don't want me to meet him?"

Michael smiles tenderly. "One of many reasons, yes."

Asher stares at their entwined fingers with a new awe that puffs up Michael's pride. They sit in silence together for a long time, the weight of revelation heavy on them both, until Asher says, "What happens now?"

"That's for Father to decide."

Asher meets Michael's gaze. "And if he decides you can't have me?"

Michael closes his eyes. "I'll be cast out."

"Like Luc—Luke."

"He says it isn't so bad."

"Well, Satan would say that wouldn't he?"

Michael laughs and Asher's lips tip up at the sides.

Asher says, "If it comes to it, if God doesn't approve of this between us, promise me you'll choose heaven."

"No."

"Please, Michael. I'll be okay. I'll even find someone else to love one day if that's what you need to hear. But don't sell your soul for me. I'm not worth it."

"Angels don't have souls—" But before he can explain more a dizzying vibration grips the room. He gasps.

It's Father.

Asher's eyes blaze with fear and the scent of ozone burns in the air.

"Don't!" Michael spreads his wings, protection from the destructive perfection of God.

"Come home, Michael."

Father's voice crushes all resistance. Asher falls into submission, eyes closed and trembling as he presses himself facedown to the floor. Surrender.

Father's summons overwhelms Michael, shuddering through his human body until he sheds it against his will, a snake stripped of skin. He's delivered up to heaven, naked at Father's feet.

"Michael, do you remember the flood?"

"Yes, Father," he whispers.

"What preceded my wrath at that time?"

"Many sins, Father. Too many to count." Michael knows what's being asked, and in the ringing, terrifying silence he stalls. Finally, he gives the answer he knows is expected of him. "Angels took daughters of men as wives and created young with them." Michael had not been among their number but he was careful not to name any names.

"My flood wiped those children from the earth."

"Yes," Michael whispers, trembling. He cannot open his eyes and he prostrates himself. "Please, Father." He does not beg forgiveness. He begs for permission.

"You have been my right hand many times, perfectly obedient, perfectly just. But the ages have changed you."

Michael feels a rising hope and he dares to reach his hands out toward Father. "Please," he begs again into the radiance that floods him.

"I have indulged you. I gave you freedom to protect your people, freedom to explore the human world."

"Yes."

"Freedom has a price."

Michael quakes.

Father is silent a long time. "There is a battle coming, Michael."

"Soon?"

A swell of visions rises within him—violence, rioting, crowds, humans screaming, crying, laughing, and a sky that breaks open as angels charge in. Fear rises, not for himself, not for the humans, but for Asher.

"Soon enough."

He sets his jaw. Asher will be protected. Michael will cover him with his wings, and may Father protect any who try to harm a hair on his head.

"I will require warrior angels by my side."

Michael searches for the purity of purpose he's known before. It's lost somewhere back in the middle ages, or perhaps in the years when the Caesars still ruled. He's empty of any desire to fight.

"You are far from the warrior I need."

"Forgive me, Father."

For I have sinned. Michael burns with shame.

Father has heard his thoughts. "There is no sin in love."

"Then why are you doing this?"

"It is not a punishment, Michael. I will always be here waiting for you. My love is eternal. But you are not human, the rules are not the same for you, and your angelic vocation comes with privileges that cannot be extended if you are no longer devoted only to me."

"Will I still feel you?"

"Not as you did. But I am always with you."

Michael trembles at the thought of not feeling Father. "If I was human, I could have you and this as well."

"You're not human. You are as I made you—fierce and strong. But you cannot remain with me and put your love above my work." A sense of peace fills Michael and he knows Father isn't angry. "Make a choice."

"Can I come back? If I change my mind, will you let me return?"

"Always."

A heavenly gong strikes quite nearby. Everything shakes. Heaven goes topsy-turvy and Michael can't move.

"Choose."

Another swell of visions fills him, this time accompanied by sensation, and it's all Asher—*why did you let me love him?*– and he's caught up in it, cresting and aching, pushing, pulling, pulsing and a sensation like orgasm catches him up and spits him out into a vision of Asher in bed asleep, his beautiful black brows and lashes against pale skin, and his human, delicate collarbones, and further down his chest, the black hair Michael likes to grip in his fingers.

Horrible aching affection holds him hard, and Michael struggles flopping like a fish at Father's feet, trying to hold the emotion back and failing. *Love.* Unangelic, far too human, tied to lust and human dreams of home and building a life.

It's love or battles, love or fighting with Father for something he doesn't understand, love or the soldier he once was?

"Choose now, Michael."

He turns toward Asher's arms, pleasure-blind and free. This, *this* is his choice.

And, just like that, he falls.

He's barefoot and naked on green grass, his house a hulking shadow behind him in the night. His wings are extended and his heart pounds. There's an emptiness at his back, as though a tether has been cut away.

He groans and folds his wings and smooths the skin in place. He waits for the crushing weight of pain, for the severity of Father's rejection to pull him down forever.

Instead pride rushes in along with a dim sense that Father is impressed with his choice, sin or no. It's not so bad at all. He chuckles and thinks he owes his brother an apology.

It's just as Lucifer said.

SEVEN

The house is not the same as he left it.

Weeds overrun the yard and vines have ventured to creep up the side. His hands tremble as he unlocks the back door with his angelic ability—relief sweeping through him that his powers appear unaffected. The light switches don't work as he makes his way through the kitchen and into the hallway. His footsteps echo as he climbs the stairs, taking his time as understanding slides through him. He took too long making his choice. It's too late.

He stands in the open door to the bedroom, moonlight pouring through the windows. The mattress is still resting on the now dusty floor. The clothes he'd discarded before making love to Asher are neatly folded in the middle of it and a note rests on top. Picking up the dry paper, he recognizes Asher's handwriting.

I waited until I knew you weren't coming back. I'm proud of you for choosing your calling. You saved me and if letting you go saves you, I'm happy to do it. Well, maybe happy is too strong a word, but I'm trying to make my peace with it. I know it's too much to hope that I'll ever see you again. I won't pine for what I can't have. You wouldn't want that. I feel blessed to my bones to have been your lover, however briefly. I don't know what to do about the house. So I'm leaving it as it is. It is better than a motel for your future assignments. Yours always, Asher

Michael drags a hand over his face and resists the urge to throw his wings out wide. How long has he been away? Father's time is not the same as earth's linear time, and he's been dumped unceremoniously without the usual finesse of a mission-driven visit.

For all he knows, it's been years.

The thought cuts through him messily, all sharp, jagged edges of loss.

Groping through his clothes on the bed, he finds his cellphone still in his jean pockets, but the battery is dead. Closing his eyes, he takes a steadying breath. There's only one place he can go in the middle of the night after falling from grace. He dresses himself and seeks out his brother's location. It's a tight squeeze through space and time, but he manages it.

"Mike! Hey, bro. It's about time," Lucifer says, grinning from his lounging position on a giant sectional sofa. He clutches an iPhone in one hand and a beer in the other, looking all too human. "Get your ass over here." He pats the seat next to him.

Michael gazes around the apartment over the surf shop, taking in the one-bedroom setup. The kitchen is small but not filthy and the counter separating it from the living room is covered in unopened mail. The walls sport posters of Lucifer's old band from a few years back, a print-shop sign reading *Hell's Parties Are More Fun*, and a few upside-down crosses. He points at the last. "Are those really necessary?"

"Ambience, baby."

Michael rolls his eyes and sits gingerly at the edge of the sectional, as far from Lucifer as he can get. "Where are the pet lions and the girls in bikinis? Where's the silk and velvet?"

"I'm trying something new." Lucifer takes a sip of his beer.

"Opulence is so *done*."

"Mm," Michael says noncommittally.

"Did dear old Dad do the deed?"

Michael scratches at his arms. Despite feeling it pulsing inside like always, he's convinced he feels his grace dying beneath his skin. "I chose."

"Hot damn. I knew you had it in you." He raises his beer in a toast. "To my fellow rebel. Shall we resume our age old fights to be the old man's favorite?"

Michael ignores the question. "Now what happens?" He remembers Asher asking the same thing. It feels only hours ago, but evidence points to it being much longer than that.

"Not much. You're the same old you. Same grace, same wings. You've just been kicked out of the club. No more celeb-style parties in the clouds. No more kissing Father's sweet-smelling toes."

Michael pulls his phone from his pocket. "Got a charger?"

"On the counter."

Michael plugs it in and hisses when the phone powers up revealing the date. "Is this right?"

"You've been topside a long time, bro."

"But seventeen months?"

"A lot's changed."

"Asher…"

"Oh, yeah. Your sweet little prince stopped by the store a month or two after you left. He nearly pissed himself, but he asked me, 'How's your brother?' It was all I could do not to devour him on the spot."

Michael whips around, snarling. "If you—"

"I didn't." Lucifer holds his hands up in surrender. "It's no fun seducing him if you're not here to watch."

Michael sits down on the sofa again and pinches the bridge of his nose, a strange sensation like a headache coming on. "What did you tell him about me?"

"That you were with Father. That's all I knew." Lucifer sniffs.

"He left then, like a bat out of hell. What did you tell him about me? I could smell his fear."

"The truth."

"What? That I'm a better lover than you? That I throw the best parties?"

Michael ignores the taunts.

"Don't worry about *me*, though. I wasn't lonely while you were gone," Lucifer says, waggling his brows. "Kept myself busy with half a dozen sailors and arranging crime sprees in Jersey."

"That's all in seventeen months? I expected more." Michael instinctively reaches out to feel Father and the silence feels as large as the universe. It fills him with yearning, a sensation he's only tasted before. Now it's consuming.

"As for your sweet meat, well, he's moved on," Lucifer says, smirking. "You gave up Father and heaven for someone who's now dating an assistant rabbi at that run-down old synagogue. Seems he's into holy types." Lucifer winks. "Choices are fun, aren't they? And consequences excruciatingly interesting."

Michael collapses back into the sofa, wiped out and aching inside. He's got angelic power. He's got his wings. He's got eternity ahead of him. But he's lost everything: Father, heaven, and Asher, too. His chest squeezes and burns. His stomach churns. The yearning swells and presses against his skin like his wings—painful, urgent. This kind of pain is new. And, yes, interesting.

"Oh, please, you're not going to cry are you?" Lucifer grimaces. "You're an angel. Take that lover-stealing rabbi down. All it takes is a flick of your finger. Stop fretting like a virgin hovering over her first fat cock."

Michael sighs. His brother is disgusting and, worse, obtuse. His throat hurts and maybe he is going to cry because his eyes burn.

"You're ridiculous," Lucifer hisses. "You *fell* for him."

"Falling doesn't entitle me to his love."

Lucifer tosses up his hands. "Now you sound like a date rape ad. 'Is she too drunk to drive? She's too drunk to consent. Don't be that guy.' Listen to me, bro, don't be *that* guy. You didn't lose heaven for a prison of honorable choices."

"For the love of Father, what is wrong with you? Have you no shame?"

Lucifer grins at Michael. The absurdity of his question floats in the air like laughter.

Michael sighs. "If he's moved on, if he's with someone he can share the seasons of life with—family, aging, death—I can't take that from him."

"You can actually."

"I won't."

"Prig."

"Satan."

Lucifer smirks. "You'll come around to my way of thinking eventually. Eternity without Father's presence is a long, long time."

"What happened to your claim he comes to visit you?"

"He does. And he's a bastard about it. He doesn't let me *feel* him. But I know he's there." Lucifer shifts around, smoothing his hands down his jeans and wrinkling his nose. "He knows I'm an addict jonesing for a fix, knows it kills me that he's right there in the same room, but I can't have him. Torture. He's a real peach, our Dad."

Michael says nothing, rubbing his eyes as exhaustion and aching sadness fills his core.

"You can stay one night. Then you have to leave. I'm not going to baby you." Lucifer points his finger at the screen on the opposite wall. "Get your lover back. Enjoy him while he lasts. Because, in the scheme of eternity, he won't last long."

A reality television show about housewives in New Jersey begins. Michael stares at it numbly, barely paying attention. They share a bowl of buttered popcorn that appears on the cushions between them. He knows what Lucifer says is true. Asher won't last long, and that's all the more reason to stay away from him. Let him enjoy his normal human life and whatever happiness he's found.

If that means Michael suffers, it's only part of Father's design.

Falling is meant to be painful.

Michael decorates his house alone.

A finger snap here and a blown breath there, and he has curtains, dishes, beds, tables, and chairs. It's attractive enough, but lonely. The dreams he's had of sharing the decisions with Asher—of seeing the man he loves choose things he admires, of learning his aesthetic—all rot on the vine, along with the dozen other fantasies he's allowed himself to concoct in defiance of Father.

Michael knows Asher will never plant the beds around the house, so he haphazardly fills the yard with hyacinth, hyssop, and honeysuckle and calls it a day.

Days pass, one into another, and he rides the time like a child on the back of a tortoise: slow and burning. The weather is hot, and his skin parches in the sun, pulls tight against his angelic form, and stings over his wings. He wants Asher, he wants Father, he wants shade, and comfort, and love.

The museum is cool when he steps inside. Footsteps echo on the tile and hushed voices murmur over the art. He's kept his mind carefully blank on the way here but once he's walking toward the painting, he can't deny why he's come.

Asher sits across from *The Archangel*, his mouth moving in a silent prayer that Michael hears above the others that always swirl around him. He's thin and strong, but he's anxious, and Michael feels that even before the heart-thumping power of seeing his beautiful face, his dark hair, and proud nose wakes him from his long wonderless sleep.

"My mother likes him," Asher prays. "My father shook his hand when he asked for mine. He wants to marry me." Asher's shoulders slump. "But I don't want to marry him." He gazes up at the painting again. "I wish this looked like you. I always thought the angel in the painting was inhumanly beautiful until I knew you. But it doesn't do the real you justice." He laughs softly. "Nothing and no one does you justice. You ruined me. And I wouldn't change that for anything in the world. But I don't want to break his heart, and I know you're not coming back. There won't be anyone else like you. No more angels for me." He laughs hard enough that he wipes at his crinkling eyes with the tips of his fingers. "Marrying him would be a good move. And he does love me. And I like him." He shakes his head, scrunching his nose and radiating with *you* ***like*** *him, Asher? Pitiful.* He covers his face with his hands.

Michael sits on the bench beside him. "No more angels for you? Are you sure about that?"

Asher goes still, swallowing hard before he drops his hands away from his face. He stares at Michael, his eyes wide and mouth wet. "You."

"You." Michael whispers back. He wants to lean forward and kiss Asher's lush mouth. It would soothe so much in him, but he holds himself back. "I've been gone a long time."

"Yeah, you have," Asher snaps, unexpected anger in his tone. It hits Michael like a whip, breathtaking and sharp. "Why are you here?"

"You prayed to me." Michael's off-balance in a way he doesn't understand. He pushes into Asher, trying to read his flesh and bones, but Asher's anger pushes back hard until Michael relents, panting. "How did you do that?" he asks.

Asher's still focused on the prayer. "I prayed to you hundreds of times in the past and you never came. I prayed to you for a year after you left. *Nothing.*"

"I was detained."

"By God?"

"Yes."

"He put you in angel jail?"

"Not exactly. Why are you angry?" Michael tries to push into Asher again and is rebuffed just as quickly.

"Because you came now. Right when I've made up my mind to

marry Stanley. Is that why you came back? To stop me?"

"I heard your prayer and I had to see you. You sounded desperate."

"Are you here—" He breaks off, bites his bottom lip, and shakes his head. "Is this a mission? Are you saving me again from another mistake?"

"I don't do missions anymore."

"I don't understand."

"I chose you."

Asher gapes. "No, you didn't. I waited for a year for you. I went back to the house every day. I paid the utility bills. I grieved. I begged. I screamed. I finally gave up."

"I'm sorry I took so long."

"You're *sorry*? Where the hell have you been all this time?"

Their whispered argument is attracting the attention of the guards and other museum guests. Michael reaches out a hand to soothe Asher since he can't calm him from within, but Asher ducks away from it.

"Father's time is different from earth's time. When I fell, he wasn't exact about when I landed. I wasn't on a mission. You were already with your rabbi and I didn't want to disturb your happiness. What I wanted? It didn't matter."

"It matters to me that I cried for you like you were dead."

Sorrow and useless regret flow through Michael. He wishes he could go back and take away Asher's pain. "I didn't hear you. When I'm with Father, I hear nothing but him." He glances around to make sure no one is watching before he closes his eyes and summons snatches of honeysuckle into his fingers. The sweet perfume fills the space between them, pungent and strong. Asher blinks rapidly before taking the sprigs from Michael's hand.

"Eternal bonds."

"Yes," Michael murmurs, and tries to push into Asher again, to sense his inner sweetness. The blocking anger retreats and he lets his angelic grace fill in the space left behind. "For you. I fell for you. And then I fell." He leaves aside all of his questions of how and why and if it's all a set up or a test. He doesn't care. He can be with Asher now that he knows he's not happy with his rabbi.

Asher gasps. "I feel you. Pushing into me." His eyes flash wide. "I've felt this before when I was with you, but I didn't know—oh!"

Michael allows his devotion to flow between them and Asher dissolves against him, the heat and weight of his body a balm for the want and yearning Michael's suffered with since he fell.

"You love me," Asher whispers.

"I told you I did."

"But you gave up—what exactly did you give up?" Asher wraps his arm around Michael's back and presses his cheek against his shoulder.

Michael supports his weight, cuddling him close. "Perfection. His, not mine. Even angels aren't perfect." He laughs softly. "Constant comfort. Boredom. But I get to keep eternity and my power and, hopefully, you."

"Me?"

"For as long as you'll have me."

"I'll age. You won't. That's creepy. I'll be some dirty old man."

Michael laughs. "Well, that's only half true. I'll never die, but I can refashion a different body. Lucifer does it every once in a while for a fresh start. I could choose older bodies so that we're more matched."

"But you don't have to do that now," Asher says, desperately, cupping Michael's cheek. "I like this one."

"I'm in no rush."

"Okay," Asher says, sitting up straight, and a smile breaking on his face. "Then I want you for as long as I live." They both feel the surge of certainty in Asher's body as he speaks the oath.

"I'm sorry I was away for so long. I hope your rabbi has been good to you."

"Assistant rabbi," Asher corrects. "He's been kind and wonderful. But, as good as he is, and as gentle, he's no angel."

Michael tugs him down for a kiss. "Let's get out of here."

"Where? Somewhere with a bed?" Asher asks.

"Of course."

"I should probably break up with Stanley first," Asher says, hesitantly.

"That can wait," Michael says. "Be with me now."

Apparently, he's no angel either.

EPILOGUE

They've spent an afternoon in Michael's bed fucking. Covered in come and sweat, they spoon up together, listening to the birds outside the bedroom window and panting softly.

Everything is perfect. Actually, everything is incredibly imperfect.

Michael's surf shop job is strange. He has to listen to Lucifer pontificate about all kinds of nonsense. His house is drafty and lonely since Asher wants to wait before moving in—a kindness in deference to the assistant rabbi's feelings, quite bruised after Asher ended their engagement. It's a good thing, but Michael can't help but to selfishly wish Asher was a crueler man in this if nothing else. But he loves him fiercely for his gentle heart.

Michael's been given to understand that Asher's father still hates him—this time for being the bastard who broke his son's heart, instead of the bastard who woke it. Sometimes in the night his wings ache so badly he cries. Everything is as far from heavenly as it can get. But none of it makes him regret his choice.

But Asher will move in soon. The surf shop job is a pleasant enough distraction. Michael can quit in the future if he wants to, and he might if Asher ever wants him to. Being around Lucifer isn't that bad, really. He's interesting at least, and keeps him on his toes.

The drafts in the house can be fixed up by human hands or angelic persuasion, and Michael's not sure why he's dragging his feet on it. Lucifer rolls his eyes and says it's because Michael wants to punish himself with petty human problems. He's probably right, and Michael smiles, taking pleasure in the mundane.

And Mr. Rosenthal will either come around to Michael's return to Asher's life or he won't. All that matters now is that Asher is smiling at him. Michael kisses the wrinkles by Asher's eyes, his heart squeezing painfully with joy.

"You make me feel old when you do that."

"You're just a whippersnapper." Michael kisses them again. "Now, tell me what you want out in the garden. Tell me how you're going to fill our flower beds."

Asher goes thoughtful. "Marjoram for joy. Myrtle for marriage."

Michael quivers inside, a bell striking deep within. Marriage. No matter what laws come and go on this earth, Asher has as good as proclaimed himself married to Michael until his death. It's an honor he doesn't know if he deserves, and a responsibility he cherishes.

"Don't get any angelic ideas," Asher says. "I want to plant it all myself. None of that magicking up plants like you did that time at the museum."

Michael nuzzles Asher's sweaty shoulder and agrees. "Roses for love?"

Asher nods and then goes solemn. "And rosemary for protection."

"But I'm not in the protection business any longer."

Asher plucks at the bed sheets. "I was thinking along the lines of protection for us."

"Are you worried about that?" Michael pushes into Asher's body and feels his anxiety. "We're safe here."

"Are we? Isn't your father angry with us? With me?"

Michael shakes his head and lays his hand on Asher's chest, feeling the steadiness of his heartbeat. Has Asher been worrying about that all of these weeks? "No. Father doesn't get angry these days." He tries to think of how to phrase it so that Asher understands. Father is awesome and terrifying, but he's no longer full of the whimsical rage he once exhibited. "He's very final in his judgements, but not wrathful. Your soul is safe. He doesn't blame you for my choice."

"Are you sure? In the Torah he's often vengeful."

"He's mellowed. In his youth, though—watch out world!"

"Literally."

"There was that flood." Michael remembers it well. The screams of the people. The orders to let them drown. No help was to be given. He frowns. "There were some nasty plagues." Locusts and sickness. The suffering of people had barely disturbed him then. Now, though, suffering gets under his skin.

"The slaughter of first born sons," Asher offers.

"I agree he's had his moments. But he's not angry about this." Michael is relatively certain. Since he no longer feels Father, he can't know for sure. But if Father wants to strike them down, he'll have done it by now. "We're safe here together."

Asher nods slowly, accepting Michael's opinion. "Let's still plant rosemary." He smiles cheekily, his eyes flashing and his voice warm with laughter. "For lust."

Michael grins, sliding his hand over Asher's chest hair, down the trail to his belly button and lower, chuckling at what he finds. "Already?"

"I want you to ride me. With your wings out."

Sex between them was always good, but with nothing between them now but naked honesty, their connection pulses, a living entity. Riding Asher's cock, looking down on his open, flushed face, Michael can no longer feel Father's stamp on Asher's bones. He only feels

Asher and it's beautiful. Asher's gentleness, forgiveness, and love rushes through him like a wave, filling the new yearning places inside.

"Let me see you," Asher says, gripping Michael's hips and pushing up into him. "Show me who I'm fucking."

Michael's wings snap open and he cries out in relief. He stretches them wide, moaning with delight, the maddening itch and burn at his back gone.

"Beautiful," Asher whispers, grinding his hips up to get as far into Michael as he can. "Michael, my angel. Come for me."

Falling, falling.

The song from the day in the bar with Lucifer pops into Michael's head as he rides Asher hard and fast, his cock straining and aching, his human flesh on the verge of maddening bliss. *Falling, falling.* Love is something with endless depths. Like the ocean. Like Asher's soul.

He slams into orgasm as hard as the earth. Hot come spurts between them and Michael drops his wings over Asher as a shelter.

"I love you," Asher says, clinging to him and shaking. "I hope God doesn't damn me for it, but I'm happy you chose me."

"I love you," he whispers. He wants to shout it to the heavens. "I'm happy I chose you, too."

The bars and missions of Mercy Street seem an eon away. Michael's no one's tool any longer. He's old, tired, and no warrior. He kisses Asher passionately, losing himself in slippery lips and hot tongue, in the eager grasp of Asher's arms and his joyful declarations of love.

He's fallen and falling, and he know he'll never stop.

THE AUTHOR

Leta Blake

Author of the bestselling book Smoky Mountain Dreams and the fan favorite Training Season, Leta Blake's educational and professional background is in psychology and finance, respectively. However, her passion has always been for writing. She enjoys crafting romance stories and exploring the psyches of made up people. At home in the Southern U.S., Leta works hard at achieving balance between her day job, her writing, and her family.

You can find out more about her by following her online:
On the web: http://letablake.wordpress.com
On Facebook: https://www.facebook.com/letablake
On Twitter: https://twitter.com/LetaBlake

ACKNOWLEDGEMENTS

Author of the bestselling book Smoky Mountain Dreams and the fan favorite Training Season, Leta Blake's educational and professional background is in psychology and finance, respectively. However, her passion has always been for writing. She enjoys crafting romance stories and exploring the psyches of made up people. At home in the Southern U.S., Leta works hard at achieving balance between her day job, her writing, and her family.

You can find out more about her by following her online:
On the web: http://letablake.wordpress.com
On Facebook: https://www.facebook.com/letablake
On Twitter: https://twitter.com/LetaBlake

Gay Romance Newsletter

Leta's newsletter will keep you up to date on her latest releases and news from the world of M/M romance. You'll also get access to exclusive content, free reads and much more. Join the mailing list today and you're automatically entered into future giveaways. All you have to do is go to the following link and let me know where to send your free newsletter!
http://goo.gl/YdcjKW

Printed in Great Britain
by Amazon